LIGHT AFTER DARKNESS

A Post Apocalyptic EMP Survival Thriller

RYAN CASEY

GET A POST APOCALYPTIC NOVEL FOR FREE

To instantly receive an exclusive post apocalyptic novel totally free, sign up for Ryan Casey's author newsletter at: ryancaseybooks.com/fanclub

CHAPTER ONE

Aoife walked towards the helicopters with Kayleigh and Rex and wasn't sure she'd felt this frigging nervous her entire life.

It was a dark night, but the sky was lit up with artificial light, which was completely fucking surreal. Blinding light from the helicopters, glaring across the grassy ground before them, contrasting the jet black of night. The deafening sound of those rotors, kicking a dusty breeze towards her. And behind her, the chatter of Robert's people. The crying. The elation and the joy.

Suddenly, everything Robert had spoken and preached about seemed totally irrelevant. Even to his most loyal adherents.

Because right here, right before them all, was an opportunity.

A chance to get away.

Hope.

Kayleigh winced as she tried to walk. Her leg was still sore from the fall from Robert's window, and in a bad way. But she didn't have to run on it anymore. She'd made it. They'd both made it. It didn't matter how exhausted and how weak and malnourished and dehydrated the pair of them felt. Because they'd made it.

They'd fought out of Robert's camp. They'd escaped his people—people who now looked transfixed by the reality of the helicopters before them.

All of that suddenly felt irrelevant.

Because the way out was here.

A chance for something better.

A chance for a new start.

But then, out of nowhere, Aoife's stomach turned. Butterflies fluttered around her chest.

What if these people weren't who she wanted them to be?

What if they weren't their saviours?

What if they were something else entirely?

Something far more malicious?

She'd fallen for false hope before. What if this was the same?

She thought about Thomas Suzuki. About his dog tag. She reached into her pocket and clutched it tightly with her shaking hands. Thought of those words underneath his name.

Order of Light.

What if this Order of Light weren't who they were cracked up to be—whoever they were?

"Aoife?"

She looked around. Saw Kayleigh staring at her. Wide-eyed, pale. And just hearing her speak, being reminded of her presence, it made her realise she had a decision to make.

But no. There was no decision about it, really. What else could she do?

There was only one way she could find out who these people were. What they wanted. And whether they were the saviours and the source of hope Aoife so desperately wanted them to be—the saviours and the source of hope they looked like.

She had to speak to them.

And she had to find out for herself.

"Come on," Aoife said, tightening her grip on Kayleigh's warm, shaking hand. "Let's go find out what they're here for."

And then, as nervous as she felt, as terrified as she was, and as much as she had no idea whether there would be good news or bad news at the end of it... Aoife, Kayleigh, and Rex walked.

She looked ahead. Squinted into the blinding light. Looked at those dark silhouettes, standing there, staring at her, staring at all of Robert's people following behind.

Or at least the ones who had chosen to follow.

Aoife looked back at them. Saw them similarly transfixed by the helicopters. Transfixed and hypnotised by this entire scene before them.

And as much as she'd fought them... she couldn't view it that way. She'd been in conflict with Robert, not his people. He was the one who exploited these people. Who thrived on their fears. Who boosted his own ego and garnered his strength from the weak. Who abused his position of power and wanted all these people to himself.

She wanted them to find a better life for themselves. She really wanted that, more than anything. Truly.

And she hoped these helicopters could provide it.

She turned back around. Saw the people up ahead. And she knew there was no time to waste anymore.

She took another deep breath, and she kept on walking.

She walked closer and closer to these people. To the helicopters. The people from the helicopters were dressed in black like Thomas had been. And they were armed, too. Armed with rifles. Fuck. What if they *weren't* on Aoife's side after all? What if they weren't on the side of the people?

What if they were here for destruction?

She gritted her teeth. Heart racing. She didn't know what they were here for. And she didn't know what any of this meant.

But there was only one way to find out.

She kept walking.

Kept walking until she was just metres away from them.

One of the people from the helicopter lowered his rifle.

He walked up to her.

Stopped, right before her.

His face was covered with a black mask.

He didn't say anything. Not at first.

And as he stood there, rifle in hand, Aoife started to get cold feet. This wasn't right. Something was wrong. Desperately wrong.

And then out of nowhere, he lifted his mask and greeted her with a smiling face.

"You'll be safe now," he said. "You don't have to worry about a thing anymore."

Everything around Aoife disappeared into a blur. She barely processed anything. Just the happiness. Just the joy.

Happiness and the joy as these people ushered her towards the helicopter.

As they helped Kayleigh and Rex get on board.

As they sat them down, offered them drinks, made them comfortable.

And Aoife could only watch through tear-filled eyes as more helicopters filled with more people. More and more people being helped. More and more people being taken away. More and more people being saved.

"Aoife," Kayleigh said.

Aoife looked at her, and she saw a smile on her face. She saw the old Kayleigh. Her old friend. Not the new, hardened, cynical woman she'd turned into.

"Thank you," Kayleigh said. "Thank you."

"For what?"

"For making me remember there is hope."

Aoife reached over, held Kayleigh's hand. Smiled, as the helicopter rose. Felt herself lifting higher. She looked outside at the darkness. At the ground below, getting further and further away.

And as she sat there, looking down, holding Kayleigh's hand, stroking Rex... she smiled.

For the first time in a long, long time, she felt herself relax.
She was going to be okay.
Everything was going to be okay.

* * *

THIS IS where these stories usually end.
Not this story.

CHAPTER TWO

oife knew her enemy was close.

It was pitch black inside this dark, dusty room. There were scraps of old newspaper trailing across the creaky wooden floor. Outside, she swore she could hear a strong wind howling away, which made it sound like someone whispering, all the time. The room reeked of damp. Unlived in. A home once occupied by a family. Four walls that would hold all kinds of stories, all sorts of history. Four walls that were home to nothing but ghosts now. Memories.

The windows were boarded up, but Aoife's flickering torch strapped to the top of her rifle made it easier to see. Every now and then, as she made her way through this room towards the door at the other side, she swore she saw movement in the corner of her eyes.

And it made sense. She knew the enemy was close. And she knew she had to be careful.

Because it was just as likely they were watching her.

She crept across these creaking floorboards. She'd seen someone run through that door up ahead; she was sure of it. Heard them when she got here, too. Heard the footsteps racing up the stairs. Heard the floorboards creaking louder. And heard that door swinging open, banging against the wall.

And she knew there was no hiding when you went through that door. The options for escape were limited. The windows were boarded up. There were no stairs or doorways through there. It was a trap, an area you just didn't want to wander into because once you did, it was already game over for you.

But there was still plenty of damage someone could do from that room. And that's something Aoife had to stay conscious of. Very, very aware of.

She reached the door. Put her shaking hand on the handle. And she got a sudden anxious vision of someone opening that door from the other side. Swinging it open and attacking her before she got a chance to take them out.

There were more risks here than there seemed at first sight.

She held her breath. Tried to listen in there for some kind of movement, some kind of sound. Usually, you could hear your enemy in there. Scrambling around. Trying to find a way out. Then trying to find a place to hide.

Then, trying to find the best place to attack from.

That's the part Aoife had to be careful of.

She'd been in this room so many times herself that she knew exactly where all the best hiding places were. Exactly where someone would be waiting to strike.

She took a deep breath, tightened her grip on the rifle, and then she lowered the handle and swung the door open.

She stepped back. Hid behind the wall. Waited for gunfire.

Nothing.

She stood there a few seconds. Usually, they'd fire straight away the second that door opened. A panicked peppering of bullets.

But the fact there was nothing here...

That told Aoife she was dealing with someone who knew what they were doing.

That she had to be even more careful.

She shuffled closer to the doorway, being conscious not to step too much into the enemy's line of sight.

When she did, she saw the darkness.

She saw the bed. Unmade. The teddy bear lying on the floor beside it, worn and spilling out its stuffed innards.

She saw the pictures of the Disney princess on the wall, right above the bed.

The little specks of rat shit on the floor.

And she saw... well.

Nothing.

She stepped into the room. Took a look to her right, immediately.

Then she stepped around the bed. Looked underneath.

Nothing.

Nobody there.

She stood up, then. Looked over at those wardrobes on the opposite side of the room.

That hunter's instinct kicking in.

If her enemy was nowhere else to be seen in here, then there was only one place they could be.

She crept over to that wardrobe. Rifle raised. Flicked her torch out, made it sound like she was walking out of the room.

She could wait. Because they'd come out of that wardrobe eventually.

Or she could just fire at the wardrobe itself.

But she wanted to see the look on their face when she shot them.

She wanted them to know they were cornered.

She walked up to the door. Slow as possible.

Stood there a few seconds.

"Your game's up," she said.

And then she opened the wardrobe door.

She went to fire right away when she stopped.

The wardrobe was empty.

There was nothing in there at all.

Aoife frowned. "What..."

A floorboard creaking to her right.

The clicking of a rifle.

"No," the voice said. "*Your* game's up."

Aoife swung around and saw the man pull the trigger before she had a chance to react.

The ball flew towards her and splattered all over her face.

"Goddamn it, Gregg," she said, rubbing the burning paint from her eyes. "You really have to go for my face? Really? Fucking prick!"

Gregg laughed relentlessly, dropping his paintball gun to the floor and planting his hands on his knees. "The look on your face. I mean, you were so confident. You really think I was just gonna wander in the bedroom of all rooms? Let you corner me? It's your weakness, that place. You always think you've got the better of someone when you hear that door open. It's your blind spot."

Aoife rubbed the stinging paint from her eyes even more. Bastard. He'd really gone and made a tit out of her. "I don't have blind spots. At least I wouldn't if you hadn't shot me in the face."

Gregg laughed some more. Then he came over with a towel. "Let me help you with that."

He wiped her face softly, sensitively. Smirking away. Dickhead. She hated losing at paintballing. Especially to Gregg of all people.

"There we go," he said. "Now how about you treat me to lunch seeing as I won?"

"You should be the one treating me to lunch after that shot," Aoife said.

"Either way," Gregg said. "Want to grab lunch or not?"

Aoife felt torn. She liked Gregg. He was nice. But there was still a reluctance there over truly connecting with someone romantically. She knew he was interested. He didn't exactly make it subtle.

But she preferred him as a friend, right now anyway. She just didn't know how to avoid hurting him when he was obviously so keen—and so sweet.

"I'll pass on lunch," she said. "But maybe we can... maybe another time?"

Gregg smiled. Nodded. He never protested, never persisted. And that made him annoyingly even more likeable. "Another time sounds great. Now come on. You look like you could do with a good shower before you step foot out of this place. Lights!"

Suddenly, the lights in the building all sparked to life.

The coverings over the windows rose up, revealing the scorching sun outside.

And outside, on the streets, Aoife saw people.

People walking along the streets, hand in hand.

People walking into shops, buying food and drinks.

People with smiles on their faces.

"Never gets old, does it?" Gregg said.

Aoife smiled. "Never."

This was her home.

This was the new world.

This was a world with *power*.

CHAPTER THREE

Aoife still had paint on her face when she met Kayleigh for lunch the following afternoon.

It was a gorgeous summer's day. They'd been lucky all spring and summer, actually. Blue skies. Warm air. The kind of day that would've been a nightmare back in that powerless world.

But things were different now.

They weren't in a powerless world anymore.

And they hadn't been for a year now.

Aoife walked down the street with Kayleigh by her side. Rex was back at home. Getting older, that dog, so a lazy sod these days. Preferred to just chill on the sofa in this heat than go anywhere with her. Used to be her shadow. Little traitor.

As she walked down the street, she never got tired of just how amazing this community was. And just how much of a distant memory the days before—or rather the days *between* power—actually were.

Twelve months ago, Aoife and Kayleigh stood on the brink of something they didn't understand. Battered. Bruised. Broken.

But then they'd found themselves looking into the eyes of a man who promised them a new home. A new home that began with a helicopter journey to the south of the country. A journey Aoife was nervous about. Because she'd been burned plenty of times by new groups in the past.

But a journey that proved so, so worth it.

A community had been set up on the south coast. It was months in the making and running for just about six months. Small, initially, but expanding gradually.

Sanctuary.

It had order. It had governance. It had food, and it had jobs, and it had a sense of hope.

But it had something else crucial.

Something that made it completely unique.

Sanctuary had power.

The origins of the electricity were somewhat mysterious. But it began with the Order of Light, a group set up prior to the blackout and tasked with restoring civilisation in case of an electrical emergency, something global governments were very quietly beginning to fear.

They worked on blueprints of communities. Ways they could restore power from the ashes if ever the worst did come to pass. They poured billions into studying advanced forms of electricity and power that could be implemented if the worst-case scenario occurred.

They'd spent months struggling to create new communities. New homes. To restore power and roll it out, all while maintaining some sense of governance and order.

And they'd done it.

Sanctuary was a success.

A success built on mysterious foundations, sure. The very electricity here—from the power source, as Harvey called it—was way, way ahead of its time. There were some kinks to it. But it seemed to be working just fine.

And at the end of the day, that's all anyone cared about.

That's all anybody needed to know.

Looking around this place, it never ceased to amaze Aoife. Seeing people whizz by on electric scooters. Seeing kids playing on game consoles. The luxury of having a hot shower. Cooking food and not worrying about fucking poisoning yourself—not all the time, anyway. So many joys of life that were once taken so for granted. Never again.

Because this place was perfect.

And, of course, there were mysteries. Aoife didn't know the technicalities of how the electricity worked. She knew there was a central "power source" that acted as a generator. She was one of the few people who'd actually been down there, right to its core, deep under the earth, and seen this bizarre, almost alien technology for herself.

Whatever it was, it kept them connected. It was the next generation of electricity, fifty years ahead of its time. Acted as a beacon for other power sources and created a wireless network of power.

Again. It baffled her. But it worked. And that's all that she needed.

But this place had been "live" for eighteen months, expanding ever since that day, and Aoife had been here for twelve of those months.

And they were twelve of the best months she'd ever experienced.

Twelve months of a bustling, lively community of just over a hundred people. But also little businesses, too. Shops she passed by. Cafes, the smell of bacon reared on the nearby farm sizzling and filling the air. A perfect little fantasy land.

And the amazing thing?

Sanctuary was just one of several districts the Order of Light was working on across the country.

Slowly but surely, normality was returning to the shores of Britain.

"You've still got a bit on your cheek," Kayleigh said.

Aoife turned around. "Huh?"

"Paint. From Gregg's gun."

Aoife shook her head, rubbed her face. She knew what innuendo Kayleigh was trying to pull. "No need to be rude about it."

"It's true, though, right?"

"What's true?"

"You two. You haven't stopped flirting for about a year now. Why doesn't one of you just bite the bullet and go for it?"

Aoife sighed. Shook her head. "There's nothing going on between us."

"That's your problem," Kayleigh said.

"Go on. Enlighten me about my problem, wise one."

"Sarcastic bitch. Your problem is you've got your head so far in the sand you don't see shit when it's right in front of you. You're so happy living in your perfect little bubble that you don't really see what's going on with other people. Not anymore."

Wow. Deep. Not entirely what Aoife was expecting. A little cutting, to be completely honest.

"What I care about is this place," Aoife said. "Doing what I can to keep it healthy. Doing what I can to help in any way I can. I'm loyal to this place. Nothing else gets a look in. We're lucky to have Sanctuary. And I won't for a moment forget that."

Kayleigh sighed. "Power's nothing compared to connection."

"Sounds like you read that in one of those shitty self-help books."

"I did, actually. And it's not shitty. I've taken a lot of comfort from it."

"Yeah, well, you keep on manifesting good shit. It's working for all of us, apparently."

Kayleigh shook her head, sighed. Aoife enjoyed tormenting her. Really, she was just happy that the Kayleigh of old was back. Well, not entirely. But when she'd run into Kayleigh in the woods a year ago—the Kayleigh who was scarred by everything that had happened with Robert—she was a hardened shell. A ghostly reminder of the girl she used to be. Somewhat ditzy, but caring and hopeful and optimistic about the world.

She was glad some of that naive, dizzy optimism had returned.

"Anyway," Kayleigh said. "You know what I'd like to manifest right now?"

"Go on."

"A delicious fry-up."

Aoife smiled back at her. Glad she'd got off the heavy shit and back into the important matters.

"You know," Aoife said. "That sounds right up my street right n..."

She stopped.

Because she heard it.

Off in the distance.

The peppering of gunfire.

She looked around, over towards the tall steel walls around Sanctuary.

Saw others looking too. The same wide-eyed looks on their faces.

"Insurgents?" Kayleigh asked.

Aoife nodded. Anger sparking up inside. "Insurgents."

Kayleigh tutted. "Looks like that fry-ups gonna have to wait a bit longer, doesn't it?"

Aoife nodded back, just as pissed.

She had to grab her gun, and she had to go deter this attack.

Just another day in the life at Sanctuary.

Or so she thought.

CHAPTER FOUR

Aoife, Kayleigh, and Gregg searched the outskirts of Sanctuary for the source of the gunfire, but so far, they weren't having much luck.

It was afternoon. Seemed to be getting hotter and hotter. All around Sanctuary, there were trees. Thick trees that hid all sorts of little communities. All kinds of secrets.

But more than anything, it held the insurgents.

Aoife's blood boiled at the mere thought of the insurgents. People who didn't like what they had at Sanctuary. They were selfish. They didn't want a world with power. They preferred living in the dark ages, where they could instil their own forms of power, their own rule. Groups like Robert's, who were more bothered about their own egos and their own followers than anything else—as much as Robert's followers had stepped into the light since reaching Sanctuary, anyway.

The woods were silent. And according to Cole, one of the watch guards, a small group had just appeared out of nowhere and fired at the wall.

"I swear, they just turned up, shot at us, and then darted," he said, shaking his head like he always did.

Aoife kept her focus on the woods ahead. "Could be an ambush. Could be trying to lure us into a trap. Either way, we need to be careful. You know how these savages can be."

"Might be a little harsh," Gregg said.

"What?"

Gregg shrugged. He didn't look at Aoife. Just kept hold of his rifle, pointing it ahead. "Calling 'um savages. They're just tryin' to survive in their own way."

Aoife rolled her eyes. Gregg was far too soft. "They attack our home. They don't want a world with power. They're terrorists, Gregg. And the more you talk like this ..."

She didn't want to finish what she was going to say because she knew it'd wound Gregg.

The more you talk like this, the less I like you.

That would be a bitter blow to Gregg's ego.

"I'm just saying," he said, with that conciliatory tone that suggested a switch of opinion, just so he didn't upset anyone. "People don't do nothing for no reason."

"That doesn't even make sense."

"Alright, Little Miss Grammar Nazi. I'm just saying... electricity ain't worth jack shit when you've got a community together. We've all seen it ourselves. Where, like, true power is."

"Have you been reading Kayleigh's self-help books?" Aoife asked.

"Hey," Kayleigh said. "Don't knock them 'til you've tried them."

Aoife shook her head, looked back ahead. "Anyway. Eyes open. We need to be careful, and we need to be smart. None of this terrorist sympathising bullshit. They attacked the walls, and there's a good chance this is some kind of trap. We need to be careful."

"Yes, boss," Gregg muttered.

Aoife scanned the woods closely. She didn't want to seem cold.

After all, she used to work in law. She'd dealt with her fair share of morally ambiguous cases.

But these people, she couldn't find any grounds for sympathising with them. They were killers. Selfish killers who spat their dummy out because the world they'd grown to love—because they could rule by bullying and live out their own narcissistic leadership fantasies—was crumbling before their eyes. Because order was returning. Because governance and power were returning.

They weren't going to go out quietly.

But they were going to go out. One way or another.

"You should really read them, Aoife," Kayleigh said, not really paying much attention to her surroundings, rifle lowered. "Seriously, there's this one by a guy called Eckhart Tolle. And he talks about how the mind is just an appearance in awareness. That the me we think we are isn't actually the centre of our universe. You know how radical an idea like that is? How much conflict could be solved if everyone just learned to wake up?"

"If it can't help me right now, I'm not sure how much good it is."

Kayleigh shook her head. "That's your problem. So closed-minded. So caught in your own bubble. So ..."

Aoife saw it right away, almost in slow motion.

"Stop," she shouted.

Kayleigh went to take another step. "What—"

It was already too late.

A trip wire.

Somewhere over to the right, a blast of bullets.

"Down!" Aoife shouted.

She fell to the ground. Listened as those bullets blasted over them. She had no idea whether Kayleigh was okay. Whether the rest of her people were okay.

Just that this was a trap.

This was a frigging trap, and they'd walked right into it.

She waited for the bullets to stop. Frigging self-help bullshit, throwing them all off guard. She'd have a word with this Eckhart Tolle bloke. See how much the mind wasn't the centre of your universe when it was being blown off your shoulders.

She waited until she was absolutely sure all was good when she rose to her feet, slowly.

Kayleigh was up.

Gregg was up.

Cole was, too.

They were okay. Phew.

"What the hell?" Cole said.

But Aoife didn't have time to answer.

She saw them.

Two of them, over in the trees.

She lifted her rifle and didn't even hesitate.

"Over there!"

She fired. Fired at them as they returned shots.

Fired as Kayleigh started firing, as Gregg started firing.

And then watched as they backed away into the woods.

Watched as they fled.

"They're off," Kayleigh said.

But Aoife wasn't having it.

She was sick of these bastards getting away.

"Not this time they're not," Aoife said.

"Aoife!" Kayleigh called.

But Aoife wasn't for dicking about.

She ran into the woods.

Ran deeper into the trees.

Ran in the direction those people had gone, as Gregg shouted for her, as Kayleigh and Cole shouted for her.

And as she got deeper and deeper, she realised she'd gone too far.

She stood there. Looking around. The woods were empty. She'd lost them. The pricks had got away.

And then she heard a branch snap, to her right.

She looked around, lifted her rifle, and she saw him.

A man. Ginger. Pistol pointed right at her.

A look of hatred on his face.

"You're on the wrong side of history, love," he said. "You're on the wrong fucking side of history."

She pulled her trigger.

The rifle jammed.

Nothing happened.

Fuck.

A smile crossed the ginger man's face. He laughed a few times, lifted his pistol, and pointed it right at her head.

"If you've got any last words... well, unlucky. 'Cause I ain't that generous—"

A bang.

Aoife closed her eyes.

Waited for the darkness.

But she was still conscious.

She was still alive.

She opened her eyes.

The ginger man lay on the forest floor.

Blood trickled out from behind his eyes.

When Aoife looked around, she saw someone walking towards her, rifle raised.

Gregg.

"You shouldn't run off like that," he said, his voice shaky.

And all Aoife could do was lift a finger. Point at the ginger man. "Still believe they're just harmless little lost souls now?"

Gregg looked around. Clearly shaken up by the whole ordeal. "That was... it was too close. Come on. Let's get back home."

He turned around. And as much as Aoife wanted to stay out here, as much as she wanted to search for the rest of the insurgents, she couldn't shift his words out of her mind.

You're on the wrong fucking side of history.

CHAPTER FIVE

"You could've died, Aoife. You should be careful. Very careful. You know just as well as I do how savage these insurgents can be."

If there's one thing Aoife didn't appreciate, it was a grilling from the leader of Sanctuary, Harvey Watson. He wasn't someone who Aoife knew very well on a personal level. Nobody did, really. Didn't need to. You didn't want to know your pilot, after all, did you? Or your doctor? No. Harvey Watson was the leader of this district and one of the main figureheads in the establishment of the Order of Light across the country. He was a pretty big deal.

And yet he was still rather humble when it came to actually interacting with him. He was surprisingly available and accessible. Kayleigh teased Aoife that he fancied her, something she outright rejected. But then he did seem to show a particular interest in her; she couldn't deny it.

"I'm okay," Aoife said. "Seriously. Gregg did good."

"But next time, Gregg might not be there. I don't want to lose one of my most valued people. People like you are so integral to everything we are doing here. You can't go putting your life in danger like that. Especially not breaching protocol. You know the rules, Aoife."

Aoife nodded. She felt like a schoolkid being grilled for disappointing her teacher. "Shoot on sight. If they flee, they flee." It was a strange rule, but it was one Aoife had respected up until today. The anger just got the better of her. The urgency. These bastards were trying to destroy their home. And it just felt wrong that they were allowed to get away with their threats for so long.

Harvey nodded. He was a large man with a constant smile to his face. Balding. Early sixties, but looking rather good for it. Had an aura of power about him. The kind of guy you immediately respected. Always dressed smart, in a black suit. Wouldn't look out of place in government before the end times.

His backstory was vague. He'd found himself in the Order of Light quite by accident. Former military, then MI5, and then a secret member of the Order of Light. A part of the early government response to clean up the mess and a big part of the rebuilding process. He never wanted to be a leader, he always said. But he'd never turn down the opportunity to help humanity where he could.

So he'd been installed as leader of this district—of Sanctuary—and since that day, he'd never looked back on this gradually expanding community, still very much in its beta stages.

"Anyway," Harvey said, standing from his desk chair. His office was quite something. All ornate pieces of furniture, expensive leather, that kind of thing. And a beautiful view from his window at the woods beyond, which Aoife often saw him staring out of at night, off into the distance. "I have a few announcements to make over the coming days. I received word of serious progress at the Welsh district. So much so that it's looking like they're going to be able to open up within weeks."

"That's great," Aoife said. The Welsh district was another one of their safe-havens. It'd had a long and turbulent set up, mostly due to issues with the technology around that area and constant run-ins with insurgents. But it finally looked promising.

"And even more immediately exciting," Harvey said, "we'll be switching the south generator on. Tomorrow."

Aoife couldn't contain her laughter. "Tomorrow? How the hell?"

"I know," Harvey said, laughing too. "But please. Keep it quiet. I want it to be a surprise that coincides with the eighteen-month anniversary. I've got my darned speech tomorrow, and as much as I don't want to rush anything at all, being able to switch the south generator on will be such a boost to everyone who's worked so hard. We're talking more light. More power. We might even be able to extend Sanctuary even further. And it's all thanks to the hard work of people like you."

Aoife smiled. Getting the south generator up and running was one of the big goals the last few months. A way of expanding power further south, extending the range, and enabling expansion and growth of this community to welcome in lots more people. Hundreds. And eventually, thousands.

But she felt a slight tension in her chest. "That's... that's really great."

"I sense there's something still bothering you, Aoife?"

Aoife didn't even realise something was bothering her. But hearing Harvey say it out loud... it made her realise that perhaps something *was* getting to her.

"It's nothing," Aoife said. "Really."

"Nonsense. If you can't speak freely, then what's the point in free speech? Tell me what's on your mind. It's the least I can do. And besides. You lot have listened to me gab on enough over the year."

Aoife smiled, lowered her head. "It's just... it's just something one of the insurgents said."

She looked up, saw Harvey watching her. Waiting.

"What did he say?"

"He said…"

She remembered his words.

You're on the wrong side of history.

And then she shook her head, smiled back at Harvey. "It's nothing. Really. I'm serious. I'll… I'd best get going."

Harvey stared at her for a few seconds. Then he smiled. Nodded. Wordless.

Aoife turned around and headed for the door.

"I really value your loyalty, Aoife. We all do."

She stopped. Smiled. Nodded.

"Thanks, Harvey. We all… we all value everything you've done for us too. Everything you are doing for us."

She walked over to the door and stepped out.

When she looked back, she swore she saw Harvey looking at her a little too closely.

But she shook her head.

Because life was good.

Everything was good here.

Wasn't it?

CHAPTER SIX

Yuri looked out at the place they called Sanctuary, and he felt a knot in his stomach.

It was dark. Late at night. He liked coming out here at night and watching this community, watching the people go about their lives inside. Happy people. Laughter. Joy.

And really, every now and then, as he stood here and watched, Yuri couldn't deny there was something remarkably alluring about it all. The promise of a life of joy. The promise of a life as close to the way things used to be as possible... yes, it was alluring. Tempting.

And seeing the light. The electricity. The power.

The reminders of what everyone used to have.

And the reminders of what everyone had lost.

The reminders of what a lucky few had restored. To enjoy, all to themselves.

The lucky and privileged few.

Bastards.

He stood there on the hill, looking down at Sanctuary. Looking at those walls. Those supposedly impenetrable walls. That's what they thought. That's what they all believed there.

Their misguided faith. Their misguided confidence that the lives they lived now were so normal and so ordinary and so perfect and with nothing to worry about.

They were going to get a wake-up call. A huge wake-up call.

And it was going to be momentous.

He took a deep breath of the cool night air. He felt groggy as hell. He didn't sleep much these days. How could anyone sleep well when they were in his position? When they had the kind of weight of responsibility on their shoulders that he had?

Nobody could sleep well when they were in his position.

He looked down at that community. He had to be careful. They were always out here, scouting, watching. Just earlier today, his people had a run-in with theirs. Two of them barely escaped with their lives. Marco wasn't quite so lucky.

Which was what had intensified the anger amongst his people. The urgency to do something. The urgency to *act*.

Well, they were going to be in luck soon. They were going to be in lots of luck.

They just had to be patient for a little while longer.

They just had to wait for that one momentous day.

The big day Yuri had heard about. That he'd overheard being discussed.

He had ears everywhere.

He looked down at that generator on the south in progress. Saw the tests they were doing on it. Saw how clearly they were getting closer to switching it on. To providing more power to more of the community. To mark their beautiful little celebration with some kind of grand announcement.

And then he looked up, right at the block of apartments that towered over the whole place, and he saw him.

The man in black. Just a silhouette from this distance. Standing there and staring out of his window. Looking out over his community. Over his town. Over his perfect little fantasy.

And Yuri felt hate.

He felt total hate.

He gritted his teeth, his heart racing, when he heard footsteps approaching from behind, crunching across the ground.

When he looked back, he saw his people.

Wayne leading the way.

"You shouldn't be this far out here," Yuri said. "It's not safe."

"Neither should you," Wayne said. "But people are getting tetchy. How much longer do we have to wait?"

"Not long."

"So you keep saying. But the last time you said that we had fifteen more people alive. Fifteen lives that've been lost because—"

"Tomorrow night," Yuri said.

His voice echoed through the silence of night. He didn't snap. Not often. But when he wanted to be assertive, he really could be.

"Tomorrow night," Yuri said, looking out over the rest of his people. All of them gathered there amidst the trees. All of them looking at him for answers. Looking at him with hope.

All of them looking at him with trust.

"Tomorrow night," Yuri said. "Everything we've waited for. Everything we've been building towards. Everything we've travelled so, so far for. It's almost time. Time for the fireworks."

CHAPTER SEVEN

It was the night of the speech, and Aoife was running late.

It was windy outside. Just typical, wasn't it? Perfect weather all summer, and on the one night they wanted it to be ideal again, the wind was up. Felt like a storm was on the horizon. Just bloody typical.

She looked into the mirror at herself as she applied her lipstick. Saw those dark circles under her eyes, all baggy and puffy. She'd always suffered from dark circles, especially when she was tired, especially when she was stressed, and especially when she was trying to make an impression.

Shit. Did she just admit that to herself?

Was she trying to make an impression?

And why couldn't she get Gregg out of her mind?

"Aoife, seriously," Kayleigh shouted. "Hurry the hell up. You're taking as long as I used to back in the day. And I know I used to take frigging ages."

Aoife rolled her eyes. She knew she was running late. She didn't want to be late for Harvey's speech or the party that followed. For the reveal of the south generator and the celebration of the eighteen months this place had been open. She didn't want to be late for any of it.

But tonight was her night off. A rare night off that she got just to let her hair down. To enjoy it. She usually worked as a guard, but she went out on hunting and scouting missions, too, as did Kayleigh. Something of a jack of all trades. Their skills in the wild were greatly valued by this place. But things were fair here, too. Time off was encouraged. Another nice perk.

"God," Kayleigh said. "Almost look like you're trying to impress someone or something."

Aoife shook her head. "Who the hell would I be trying to impress?"

"Oh, I dunno. Who could you possibly be trying to impress?"

Bitch. Aoife wanted to tell her to shut the hell up. But probably best to just ignore her.

"Wow. You're even blushing."

"I'm not blushing."

"You're *definitely* blushing."

Looking in the mirror, Aoife realised she was most definitely blushing. Hell, she didn't even have to look in the mirror to know that; she could tell from the burning sensation across her face. And the more Kayleigh banged on about it, the more she felt her cheeks getting hot. Her hand shook as she tried to apply the last of the lipstick. Her pulse became more detectable, in her chest and her neck. She felt hot. Really hot.

"Okay," Aoife said. "Maybe I am blushing."

Kayleigh rolled her eyes, shook her head. "What's the big deal, anyway?"

"What do you mean?"

"I mean... you and Gregg. Like, you're both adults. And you're acting like kids."

"Why are you so obsessed with me and Gregg?"

"I'm not obsessed with you and Gregg. Don't start your deflecting thing."

"My 'deflecting thing'?"

"That thing where when someone criticises you, you deflect the problem onto them."

"I do that? Really?"

"Yeah, Aoife. Yeah, you do. And you always have."

Wow. Rude. But then Aoife figured that's why she got on with Kayleigh so well. She didn't sugar-coat things, especially not anymore. She was honest. Sometimes brutally so. And in this world, that was a quality Aoife had to value.

"I mean," Aoife said. "Would it really be so wrong?"

Kayleigh lowered her head. Now *she* was blushing. "I... I mean, no, I guess."

"What's up?"

"Nothing's up."

"Before, you were all cheerleading and obsessing about Gregg and me. Now I've asked you if you think it'd be a good idea, and suddenly you're acting all weird."

"I'm not acting weird. You're acting weird."

"Who's deflecting now?" Aoife said.

Kayleigh smirked. "Touché."

She lowered her head. Walked over to Aoife.

"Look. I just... I just want you to be happy. I know how much this place means to you. But I want you to have fun, too. I just... I don't know. Gregg? Really?"

"What's wrong with Gregg?"

"What's wrong with him? Nothing's *wrong* with him. But that's kind of it, isn't it? He's just sort of... alright? And you're... well, you're kind of gorgeous."

Aoife looked back in the mirror. She never saw herself as gorgeous. And she seemed to be ageing more by the day.

"Maybe I'm at that time of my life where 'alright' is what I want. Especially after Jason. I'm done with drama."

She looked around at Kayleigh, still in disbelief that she'd actually said what she'd said, admitted what she'd admitted, and been willing even to entertain a relationship with another person.

Someone who wasn't Max...

She swore she saw a hint of sadness in Kayleigh's eyes.

"Now come on," Aoife said. "I'm ready."

Kayleigh opened her mouth as if she was going to say something else. Then she just nodded and smiled. "Come on, Cinderella. Let's get you to the ball."

They walked out of Aoife's house and onto the streets, where the happy masses of Sanctuary flooded towards the podium where Harvey was due to give his speech.

As Aoife looked over at the hills in the distance, she couldn't shake the feeling that this was just like that New Year's Eve when the power went out.

She shook her head. Smiled.

That was the past.

This was now.

Everything was going to work out just fine.

Right?

CHAPTER EIGHT

oife stood right at the back of the crowd in front of the podium and wished she'd been a bit quicker getting ready.

Especially 'cause she was miles away from Gregg.

It was dark. The wind had picked up even more, but the rain seemed to be holding off. If this was a storm, then it looked like they might be in luck. Or at least that's how it seemed, anyway. It could turn at any minute, at a moment's notice. Aoife knew that was inevitable. Not just with the weather, but in life in this world.

Well. Life *before* Sanctuary, anyway. Sanctuary had brought a permanence. Sanctuary had changed everything. Things felt safer now. More secure now.

And that's the way things were going to stay.

She looked around at all the people gathered. This large crowd, hundreds of them here. It was all very tight-knit and close quarters. The smell of aftershave and perfume filled the air. The sound of laughter, of happiness. A slight stickiness to the ground where booze had been spilled. But the good thing with boozy piss-ups these days? Nobody ever seemed to get mad or angry anymore. Everyone was just... content. Even when they were pissed, scuffles didn't go on for long. It's like being saved by this place had changed everyone. Rewired everyone to be more grateful rather than... well, rather than being dicks, frankly.

People weren't suffering anymore. Things were good here.

And things were about to get a whole lot better.

She looked around for the front of the crowd, tried to find Gregg. She knew he was up top somewhere, but she couldn't see him anymore.

"Getting worried about your boyfriend?" Kayleigh asked.

Aoife felt her cheeks heating up again. "I'm just seeing if there's any way we can get closer to the front."

"There was a way of getting closer to the front. It's called having your makeup done earlier than the last frigging minute."

"Not a lot I can do about that now," Aoife said.

"Well, it's your loss. I'm not the one trying to *seduce* someone."

Aoife tutted, getting a bit sick of Kayleigh's bullshit now. She liked Gregg. Time to actually face it. She didn't know why, and she didn't know what drew her to him, but she liked him, and she couldn't deny that.

But right now, tonight, it was about hearing what Harvey had to say. What he had to announce. Celebrating.

And then she could worry about Gregg later. What was she worried about anyway? That he was going to just ditch her for some other woman in the space of a night?

She had to pull herself together. She wasn't a teenager anymore. She was in her frigging thirties. Didn't feel like it. Did anyone ever feel older than their early twenties? Did anyone feel like time was moving at an appropriate speed? Shit. Guess that's how mid-life crises happen.

She took a deep breath and focused on Harvey. Watched him step onto the podium. Heard the claps, heard the cheers.

"Ladies and gentlemen," he said, the microphone screeching a bit, making everyone wince. "Seriously," he said. "Be grateful. If someone told you you'd hear a microphone screeching a year ago, you'd snap their hands off."

Laughter. More applause. More whooping. He had a way, Harvey. A way of getting everyone to feel motivated. To feel optimistic. To feel positive.

He was the perfect leader.

"We gather here today to celebrate eighteen months. Eighteen months since we opened our doors. Eighteen months since this new world well and truly began. A perfect eighteen months. And I want to thank each and every one of you for making it so perfect. I know it's not been easy for everyone. I know it's an adjustment period. And I know there are still those on the outside who wish us harm."

A chorus of boos, then. A chorus Harvey allowed to ring out for a few moments.

"But," he said. "We have one thing those outsiders don't have. We have power. And because we have power... we have strength."

A series of claps. Of applause. More cheering.

"Now, I had a speech written. But I don't want to bore you to death. Actions speak louder than words, right? So, it's on that note that I bring you some very, very special news."

A few mutters. Whispering. People wondering what the hell he was talking about.

He looked right at Aoife, and he smiled. Right into her eyes, just for a second.

"I'm delighted to announce we're switching on the south generator. Tonight."

An eruption of cheers. People throwing their drinks in the air. Jumping around manically.

"Shit," Kayleigh said. "That's what he told you? That's what he's been hiding from you?"

She saw the elation in Kayleigh's eyes. She saw the happiness on all the faces of all the people.

Harvey was beaming. "And with power to the south, we can begin to expand. We can begin welcoming more people into our home. We are leaving the trial stages and stepping into a brave new world. Together."

People clapped and roared with delight and hope.

Aoife saw her perfect, happy community, and she couldn't help feeling the joy.

She looked at the front of the crowd, right by the podium, and she saw Gregg standing there, looking right back at her.

He looked into her eyes, and he nodded. Smiled.

And she looked back at him and nodded and smiled, too.

She'd go over to him soon.

She'd go over, and she'd celebrate with him.

Because she had to admit it. She couldn't run from it. Couldn't hide from it anymore.

She liked him.

She really quite liked him.

"So, join me," Harvey shouted. "Join me over at the south district. Join me to witness the switch on. Join me to—"

It all happened so fast.

Aoife heard a bang.

A huge bang up ahead.

Or behind her.

Or all around her.

Or...

She looked up ahead. Heard a few screams. A few giggles. Sounded like fireworks.

Only...

The way Harvey looked back from the podium.

The way he looked back, towards the wall.

Over at the smoke.

"The south. We're under attack. We're under—"

Nobody had a chance to do anything.

Nobody had a chance to scream.

Because at that moment, the podium exploded, and Aoife went flying back into the darkness.

CHAPTER NINE

One second, Aoife was on her feet.

The next, she was flying through the air.

She landed against the solid ground. Smacked her head against it. Hard.

Ringing in her ears.

A flash of light filling her vision.

She lay there on her back, tasting blood. She couldn't hear through the ringing in her ears. Couldn't see much for the remnants of that burning light filling her vision.

But as she lay there, heart racing, pain splitting across her head, staring up at the sky, she knew exactly what she'd seen.

And she knew how wrong it was.

She lifted her head, feeling dizzy, shaky, and looked ahead.

When she saw the scene in front of her, she felt a sinking feeling that she hadn't felt in a long, long time.

The podium was covered in flames. There were people scrambling off it. Being escorted away. Flames rose from the remains. Smoke rose into the air.

But it was what was in front of the podium that made Aoife's skin crawl.

Up ahead, the crowd that was gathered before were flattened. Loads of them were dead on the ground. Bleeding out from gaping holes in their necks. Or lying there, eyes staring emptily up at the sky. Some of them were barely even in one piece anymore.

And as Aoife stood there and stared, the ringing in her ears turned into screams. The screams of people staggering around her. Some of them limping and wounded. Some of them just unrecognisable with the terror in their eyes. Panic. Chaos. Confusion. It reminded her of the estate over a year ago. Losing Max. The conflict with Grace...

She thought of Kayleigh. Looked around for her. She was right beside her a moment ago. Or at least it *felt* like a moment ago. Maybe she'd passed out. Maybe the fall had knocked her unconscious.

She had to reach her.

She had to find her.

Then she had to get them both the hell away from here.

She searched through the pile of bodies, panicked people racing past her, almost knocking her to the road. She didn't even know if the attackers were still close. That's what it felt like—like they were under attack. Every now and then, she swore she heard gunfire.

And her instincts told her to get her gun and help defend this place if that's what needed doing.

But even greater instincts screamed at her to do something else entirely.

To find Kayleigh.

To find her friend.

She couldn't leave her behind.

She scrambled over the bodies. Faces of people she recognised. Faces of friends. And she couldn't shake the fear or the denial. This couldn't be real. This couldn't be happening. This had to be a nightmare. It just had to be.

Because things like this didn't happen at Sanctuary.

This was their safety.

This was their home.

Things like this weren't supposed to happen here.

She searched even more for Kayleigh. Sifted through the bodies. Pushed past the crowd, which was thickening, suffocatingly so. People screaming. People covered in blood. The stench of blood so strong in the air. Children wailing for their parents. Dogs barking.

The smell of flames and the heat of fire and the stench of smoke...

This was a nightmare.

It couldn't be happening.

"Kayleigh," Aoife shouted.

But her shout was weak. Half-hearted. Because deep down, she had a bad feeling. A horrible feeling in the pit of her gut.

A horrible, sickening feeling that she didn't want to face.

But a feeling she couldn't deny.

A feeling that she was already too late.

She looked around and went to shout for Kayleigh again when she saw someone lying there right up ahead.

The blonde hair.

Face down. About Kayleigh's size.

Aoife shook her head. "No. Not you. Please, not you."

She didn't want to walk towards her. Didn't want to see.

But she knew she had no choice.

She went to take a step, a familiar feeling growing inside. A sense of inevitability that she'd felt so many times before. Everything around her dropped into the background. Nothing seemed to matter. Everything seemed to fade into insignificance. Nothing made any clear sense.

Just this woman, lying face down on the ground.

"Kayleigh," she said. "Please. Not you. Not you."

She went to take another step towards her when she felt a hand on her shoulder.

"Aoife?"

She turned around, and she saw her.

Kayleigh stood there, right before her.

A small cut above her left eye.

But on her feet.

Alive.

She was okay.

"Kayleigh," Aoife said, launching herself at her. Hugging her. Holding her amidst all the chaos. "You're okay."

"Aoife."

"You're okay."

Kayleigh hugged her back. But then she pushed her away, just slightly. There was something wrong. She could tell from the look in Kayleigh's eyes.

"What is it?" Aoife asked.

Kayleigh lowered her head.

"Kayleigh? What is it?"

Kayleigh lifted her head then turned to the front. Right by the podium. "The people up top. I don't think... I don't think any of them made it."

Aoife didn't understand what Kayleigh was getting at initially. She was so caught in the adrenaline of the moment that it didn't quite click.

And then it hit her.

"Gregg," she said.

She started running towards the front of the crowd.

"Aoife!" Kayleigh shouted.

But there was no stopping her.

She had to get to Gregg.

He was up top.

The last thing Aoife remembered before being blown back was looking at Gregg. Seeing him at the front, smiling.

And then...

No.

She kept on running.

Trampled over bodies and felt so fucking guilty about it.

Pushed past the tight crowd of people heading in the other direction, so many people that she was suffocated by the smell of booze, sweat, fear.

She pushed and pushed and kept on going until she reached the front of the crowd, and she saw him.

He was lying there on the ground.

Staring up at the dark sky above.

Wide-eyed.

Spluttering blood.

"Gregg," Aoife said.

She ran to his side.

When she got there, she realised it was already too late for him.

There was a huge chunk of metal debris through his throat. Another, right through the middle of his chest.

And as she sat there beside him, all she could do was hold his hand.

Hold his cold, shaking hand and be there with him.

He looked into her eyes. A tear rolling down his face. A smile on his blood-soaked face.

"I'm sorry," she said, as he spluttered away, as she tried to hold back her tears. "It's going to be okay. Don't worry. It's... it's all going to be okay."

She had no idea how long she held his hand and comforted him.

But eventually, Gregg stopped spluttering, and the light in his eyes went out.

CHAPTER TEN

Aoife stood in the middle of the graveyard.

It was afternoon, but it was dark already. Thick black clouds overhead. Rain lashed down from above, cutting through the stuffy, humid air. The storm that threatened to rear its head yesterday was well and truly here now. And it seemed fitting. Fitting after everything that happened last night. Fitting, after everything had fallen apart.

Aoife looked at the church up ahead. Looked at the old headstones sitting there amidst the muddy grass. And she saw the survivors all standing around. All dressed in black. Heads lowered. Eyes down.

It felt like the bubble they had been living in for the last year had well and truly burst.

And after how it'd gone down... Aoife wasn't sure they'd ever be able to return to that bubble again.

Everyone was silent. They were gathered here just to pay their respects. There were holes in the ground where they'd buried some of the bodies. Or at least, what remained of the bodies, anyway. It wasn't like they could do anything on the main square, where the explosion at the podium had erupted. Because there were still remains there. There was still blood on the streets.

And there were still memories.

Memories of the blast.

Memories of the screams.

And memories of the look in Gregg's eyes as he lay there, dying.

In the middle of the graveyard, standing there covered in cuts and bruises, Harvey stood. He'd survived. A miracle, considering how close he'd been to the explosion. Had to be dragged from under the rubble and survived without even a broken bone.

That was one positive, at least. One bright spark in the insufferable darkness.

At least they still had their leader.

At least they still had Harvey.

He looked up at the crowd that was gathered. In the background, Aoife could still hear crying. The grieving cries of so, so many. There was a depression hanging over Sanctuary. And it was only going to get even stronger as the days went on.

As the shock rose.

And all Aoife could think about were those insurgents, who must've breached the walls, somehow. Who must've planted a bomb. Attacked the south wall and destroyed the south generator, then left without a trace. A suicide attack, some speculated—but that didn't explain the attack on the podium. Someone on the inside? The thought made Aoife sick.

It felt wrong. It filled Aoife with anger. And while she knew to be wary of a lust for vengeance nowadays, she felt nothing but hatred towards the insurgents. Nothing but detestation.

Because they were selfish. They were selfish and ruthless, and they'd crossed a line.

They'd been knocking at the door for far too long, and finally, they'd crossed a line.

"I don't know where to even start," Harvey said.

His voice didn't fill Aoife with the usual reassurance.

The illusion of safety and comfort had been shattered completely. It's like what'd happened had totally broken things. And she wasn't sure how things were going to go back.

"We're still unsure of the numbers exactly," Harvey said, his voice shaking, the remorse and the pain clear to hear. "We're still finding more today. But... but every one of those people was a credit. They were a credit to this community. And they are a great, great loss. And I am so sorry."

"Sorry's not enough," someone shouted.

Aoife looked around. Everyone did, clearly a little shocked to hear any kind of mutiny against Harvey. Everything was usually so coherent here. People didn't disagree with one another, and when they did, it was politely and diplomatically.

It was Remi. His eyes were bloodshot. She could see tears glistening on his cheeks. He looked mad. Really mad.

And Aoife could sense anger in Remi's voice.

She could sense anger deeper within the group.

A sense that something was going to change.

"I know apologies can't bring anyone back," Harvey said.

"But killing the fuckers who did this might stop anything like this happening again," Remi barked. "Because it should never have happened in the first place. Never."

Harvey stood there, eyes wide, staring out at the crowd. And Aoife felt bad because she could feel the atmosphere shifting. She could feel the mood shifting. From grief to anger.

And she felt it herself.

Anger that something hadn't been done sooner.

Anger that the insurgent threat hadn't been dealt with before now.

Not a mere lust for revenge. But a feeling that this should not have been allowed to happen. And that it should never be allowed to happen again.

"Those terrorist fucks have fucked with us for too long," Remi shouted. People clapping along. Cheering. Clearly well on board. "And we can't let it go on. Because if we let it go on, we'll lose more people. It'll happen again. We need to send out a message. More than a message if we can. We've dicked around with diplomacy for so long. And my wife is dead. So many people are dead."

Aoife heard the claps. She heard the applause. She heard the angry roars.

And all she could do was look at Harvey as he stood there, staring out at his people, a single teardrop rolling down his face.

He closed his mouth. Nodded. Waited a while without saying a thing.

"I tried to avoid this day," he said. "And I did it because I thought I was doing what was best. Truly."

Another pause. The crowd waiting on with bated breath.

"But now I see something more needs to be done."

A mumble amongst the crowd.

"Now, I see it's no longer can the insurgents terrorise us."

The mumble becoming shouts. Cheers.

"It's time to do something different. For the ones we love. It's time to go after them. And it's time to wipe them out. Once and for all."

CHAPTER ELEVEN

Aoife and Kayleigh stood outside Harvey's office and waited to be invited inside.

It was late. She had no idea why she and Kayleigh had been called up, especially so late. The plan was to launch an attack on the insurgents as soon as possible, but realistically that meant waiting until tomorrow at least. Harvey and some of his closest were putting a plan together. It seemed like the entire community of Sanctuary was channelling their grief into their vengeance. Aoife knew the perils of going down that road. She thought of Grace and all the pain revenge had got the pair of them into.

But this time felt different. This time, the actions of the insurgents felt totally unjust.

And it wasn't just about revenge. It was about protection, too.

Protecting this community from future attacks.

And if that meant taking the insurgents out, then that's what had to be done.

Aoife stood in the corridor outside Harvey's office, Kayleigh by her side. It felt like she'd been standing here and waiting forever. Besides, neither of them knew why they were here. They'd just been picked out at random and told to come here because Harvey wanted to speak to them about something. He had a job for them. A very important job that he wanted to keep quiet. Something he could trust them with.

Aoife wondered what it could possibly be. She appreciated Harvey's trust. But still, there was an uncertainty over what all this was about.

She stood there. Nervous. Tired. Shaking a little after everything that had happened. She could still see flashes in her mind of Gregg and the look in his eyes—the dead look in his eyes. The fear, in his final moments.

And it filled her with anger. Filled her with pain.

But then she took another deep breath. She had to stay strictly on task here. She couldn't let vengeance get the better of her. She couldn't let it cloud her judgement. Not again.

She heard a creak up ahead and saw Harvey at the door.

He looked pale. Exhausted. He was usually so pristine, but his hair looked greasy and his shirt untucked and scruffy. Actually looked kind of pitiful. Didn't give off the biggest leadership vibes, that was for sure.

"Aoife. Kayleigh. Glad you could make it. Come inside."

He held up an arm and gestured for them to enter. They both went into his office, which smelled of sweat. There was a sleeping bag on the floor by his antique oak desk. Looked like he'd been holing up in here while planning the response.

"I don't want to go home until I've got a proper plan in place," Harvey said, closing the office doors. "And if that means staying here until next Christmas ... then that's exactly what I'll do."

"You should get some rest," Aoife said. "You won't think as clearly without it."

"I can get by on a few hours just fine," Harvey said. "Besides. I'm not sure I deserve much sleep right now."

He lowered his head, and Aoife saw the guilt all over him.

"You need to stop blaming yourself for what happened."

"How can I not blame myself? I'm the one who's called for diplomacy. I'm the one who called for watchful waiting. I'm the one who belittled the insurgent threat. Who undermined it completely. And now look. People are dead. People are dead, and the south generator is destroyed too, and that's on me."

Aoife didn't know what else she could say to reassure Harvey. Truth be told, it looked like he'd already made his mind up about all this. And Aoife knew it was nigh on impossible to get through to someone when they'd already made their minds up. Knew that much damned well from first-hand experience.

"I'm sorry you feel that way. I know there's nothing I can say to change your mind. But... but all I can say is there's nothing we can do but channel it into our next step. Which is what it looks like you're doing."

"And that's exactly why I've invited you here," Harvey said, nodding along. "Soon, we'll launch an attack. But the problem is, we still don't know exactly where these people are located, their numbers, or anything like that. I've tried requesting support from some of our other Order colleagues, but we're on our own with this one. Self-sustaining, you know the spiel they usually give. So we need to tread carefully. They attacked us in a way we didn't think they were capable of. That should be a warning sign in itself."

"Where are you going with this?" Kayleigh asked.

"I want you two to go out and find these people tonight. I'm asking you because I trust you. You're loyal. And you can be relied on. And if you can scout them out, if you can locate them... then maybe we can understand more about these people before they become a problem again."

Aoife felt a nervous tension in her chest. Everything was suddenly getting very real.

"I'm asking you both because, like I say, I trust you both. And I trust that you'll act appropriately. That you won't be poisoned by these folks. It's clear someone intercepted us. I mean, they must have. Whether someone on the inside or a suicide bomber... we're still trying to work that out. I don't want this to happen again. And I trust you both."

"I don't see what good this will do," Kayleigh said.

Harvey frowned. "What?"

"What if something happens to us out there? There's only two of us. And it's like you said. We've no idea how tough this group is. What if we walk right into a trap?"

"I don't want to be blunt," Harvey said. "But there's going to be risks associated with every inch of this operation. I'm asking you two because you are capable. And because you are loyal, and I can trust you. We're going to lose a lot of soldiers in this battle. We're already losing them. But this way... maybe we can minimise the damage."

Aoife saw Kayleigh shake her head. She clearly didn't like the way Harvey was talking about this.

But she heard Harvey's words, saw the way he looked at her, and she knew what he was saying.

"This will help Sanctuary. This will help secure our future. Isn't that worth fighting for?"

She swallowed a lump in her throat.

Took a deep breath.

Then, she nodded.

"I'm in."

Kayleigh looked around at her. Eyelids twitching.

Harvey half-smiled. He looked a bit more alive now. "Good. Thank you. Thank you so much. Kayleigh?"

Kayleigh looked at Aoife. Then back at Harvey. And as much as it looked like she wanted to stand up, to speak her mind, she lowered her head, and she nodded. "Me too, I guess."

Harvey's smile widened. "Good," he said. "I'm so, so grateful for you both. Let's get you loaded up and get you out there as soon as possible. Time is of the essence."

He walked up to Aoife, put a hand on her shoulder.

"It's time to save our community."

CHAPTER TWELVE

A oife and Kayleigh walked into the night in search of the insurgents, but truth be told, they weren't having much luck.

The night sky was clear and filled with stars. The moon shone down brightly from above. Made Aoife feel somewhat exposed, even though she was protected by the trees. They'd been through towns. They'd been through fields. It felt like they'd been everywhere. And still, they hadn't found a trace of the insurgents.

It was like they were invisible. No footprints. Nothing.

Which felt impossible, considering just how big an attack they'd launched on Sanctuary.

Up ahead, Aoife could see caravans. An old site, slap bang in the middle of the woods, right by a lake. Hot tubs that had gone unused for a long time, the water from them smelly and stagnant now. Unkept gardens, grass rising high. Boats lying on their back in the lake water, bobbing along the surface. She wished Rex was here. He'd love a dip in that water. Although probably not the best idea when they were trying to keep a low profile.

"Let's face it, Aoife," Kayleigh said, sighing. "We've not a clue where they are, and we aren't gonna find them any time soon."

Aoife ignored her. Kayleigh's whinging was annoying her. They needed to stay focused. Focused on the plan.

"Harvey won't be mad," Kayleigh said. "If it's upsetting him you're worried about."

"I'm not worried about upsetting Harvey."

"Really? You're his little teacher's pet."

"That's not true."

"Of course, it's true. Why do you think he asked you to do this in the first place?"

Aoife shrugged. "He asked you too."

"Probably just to keep you in check. But honestly... this was your call, coming out here. I never liked the idea. Something I don't like about it at all. Just feels... dangerous."

Aoife looked around at the empty caravans. This place had clearly been abandoned long ago. "Everything about this is going to be dangerous. There's no part of this process that won't be dangerous. But Harvey is right. We're out here because we need to track the terrorist bastards down. We need to know exactly what we're dealing with. And if we can prevent anything like that happening again... then that's exactly what we have to do."

Kayleigh looked at her, then turned away. In that way that told Aoife there was definitely something still on her mind.

"What?"

Kayleigh shook her head. "I didn't say anything."

"You didn't have to say anything. I know that look on your face."

"I just..."

"Go on. Spit it out."

Kayleigh sighed. "Sometimes I just wonder how far you'd go even if the truth was staring you in the face."

"What's that supposed to mean?"

"It doesn't mean anything. I just... I dunno. There's something about you that reminds me of how I was. With Robert."

Aoife laughed a little. "You're saying Harvey's like Robert? Really? Is that what you're implying here?"

"I'm not saying that at all. I'm just... All I'm saying is, be careful when you stop questioning things. When you start only accepting the answers right in front of you. Because that's dangerous."

Aoife felt angry. How dare Kayleigh even imply Harvey was like Robert in any way. Robert was a vicious cult leader who was all talk and no end product. Harvey was their saviour. He'd saved them from the darkness, and he'd given them power. He'd given them safety. And he ran by democracy, not with lies.

"Look," Kayleigh said. "All I'm saying is... let's just take our time here. If we don't find anything, we don't find anything. We fall back. Get some rest. We could definitely do with some rest, that's for sure."

"I don't want rest. Not while people are dead. Not while there's blood on the hands of these insurgents. I won't rest until I find them. And neither should you. Because every second they're out there... they're a threat. And that can't go on."

Kayleigh looked back at her. Wide-eyed. Almost like she was crazy, which Aoife still couldn't wrap her head around because she wasn't the crazy one here. If anything, Kayleigh was, by even *implying* Robert and Harvey were similar.

"If you want to go back, you go back," Aoife said. "But I'm here to do what I was asked to do. For our community."

She walked past Kayleigh, kept on going, not looking back, not once.

"You know what?" Kayleigh said. "Maybe I will go back."

"You do that."

"You'd really let me? On my own?"

"You're a big girl. You can look after yourself."

"Wake up, Aoife."

Aoife stopped. Looked back.

Saw her standing there, shaking her head.

"What did you say?"

"I'm sorry you're feeling the way you're feeling about what happened yesterday. I'm sorry about Gregg. I'm sorry about all of it. But you need to face it. The place we thought was perfect wasn't perfect at all. It was vulnerable. It *is* vulnerable. Just like everywhere else. And that's how it's always going to be. No matter how many terrorist fucks we take out in the process. That's the nature of the world before the power went out. That's life. Nothing is permanent. It's about time you woke the fuck up and realised that."

Aoife's cheeks burned. There were so many things she wanted to say to Kayleigh. So many ways she wanted to physically explode.

She went to open her mouth to lambast her when she heard something.

Close by, cutting through the silence.

Voices.

CHAPTER THIRTEEN

Aoife heard the voices, and she knew they weren't alone.

She stood there in the darkness of the caravan site. The moonlight bounced off the lake water in the distance. And as she listened to those voices, she knew it could be absolutely anyone at all.

But there was a place deep down that told her she knew who this was.

Exactly who it was.

The insurgents.

Somehow, she just knew it was them. It had to be them.

They were close.

She turned around. Looked past the caravans. Looked into the darkness of the woods. Kayleigh stood there with wide eyes, too. Suddenly, their argument earlier slipped into irrelevance. It felt like it didn't matter at all.

Because they weren't alone.

And every instinct in Aoife's body was screaming at her that these were the insurgents. They had to be the insurgents.

She stood there, frozen in the woods. Listening as those voices got louder. As those footsteps got closer.

And she knew they needed to lay low.

Because it sounded like there were a few of them.

Whoever they were, there were a few of them.

"Behind the trees," Aoife said. "Now!"

They both bolted over to the left, over to where the trees were thicker, away from the caravans. And part of Aoife wished they'd stayed by the caravans now. Wished they'd hidden under one, or inside one.

But fuck, time was of the essence, and she'd chosen the trees. Chosen the woods. There was no going back on that. Not now.

She threw herself behind a tree. Stood there, right behind it. Holding her breath. Heart racing.

Kayleigh stood behind the tree beside her. Staring at her. Venom in her eyes, like she couldn't quite believe she was still here, that the pair of them were still here—both fully aware they were in the shit. Deep, deep shit.

Aoife held her breath and stood there, very still, gripping on to her rifle. She didn't hear anything. Where were they? Had they walked on?

She was about to peek around the tree when suddenly, she heard the voices get clearer.

"But we have to be careful, Vernon," a woman said. "You've seen their numbers. Any wrong move and they'll be onto us."

"Bullshit. They wouldn't dare."

"Either way... the sooner we get back to Liskeard, the better."

Aoife stood there behind the tree as these footsteps passed, listening to them and the voices. She didn't know how many of them there were, but there were definitely more than the two talking.

All she could think about, unable to peek around the tree to look, was that location.

Liskeard.

That must be where their camp was.

But they still needed to be sure these were the insurgents. They couldn't know for definite. Not yet.

As much as something inside screamed at Aoife that it was most definitely them.

"Rather stick around here for a while if I'm honest," the man —Vernon, presumably—said. "Only downside is we didn't get to stick around and watch the looks on their faces. Listen to their screams. Only thing that coulda made it all better."

The woman tutted. "Sicko."

They carried on speaking, but Aoife didn't hear their words anymore.

All she did was grip her rifle tighter.

Her anger swelling inside.

Rage.

Fury.

These were the insurgents, for definite.

It was them.

And she needed to do something about them. She couldn't just let them walk away.

She needed to stop them.

She peeked around the side of the tree and saw them.

Five of them. All passing through the caravan site. All walking alongside the lake.

All armed.

"Aoife," Kayleigh whispered.

Aoife shook her head, waved her off.

"We know it's them," she said. "And we know where they're heading. Liskeard. That's where they said. Come on. Let's get back."

But Aoife wasn't for ending this mission right here.

She wasn't for giving up.

"Aoife!"

But Aoife wasn't listening.

She was getting to these people.

She was following them.

There were only five of them. And they had no idea they were being watched.

They could find something out from them.

They could maybe even deal with them.

She stepped out from behind the tree. Walked, slowly as she could. Clenching her rifle in her shaking hands, gripped tightly. Up ahead, she saw those people. Those insurgent bastards.

She could see Gregg's dead eyes staring back at her as she moved towards them, as she got closer.

She could feel her anger getting stronger and stronger, even though she told herself to suppress her urge for revenge.

She got closer when she felt a hand against her arm.

She looked around. Saw Kayleigh standing there, holding her, shaking her head.

"Don't do this, you fucking idiot. Don't you dare."

But Aoife yanked her arm away.

"This is for our community," she said.

"We might not have a community if we don't get back and tell Harvey where they're located. Now come on. Snap out of it."

Aoife wanted to listen to Kayleigh. She got it. Fully.

But then she remembered what that man, Vernon, said.

About wanting to hear the screams.

Gloating about the pain and the misery they'd caused.

And she knew she couldn't just sit back.

She turned around and walked towards the group when suddenly, she heard something snap right beneath her feet.

A branch.

A loud echo, right through the darkness.

Right through the silence.

She looked up. Hoping it wasn't as loud as it seemed to her. Praying.

And then she saw something that filled her with dread.

The insurgents turned around and looked right at her.

CHAPTER FOURTEEN

Aoife saw the insurgents staring right at her, and the whole world felt like it crumbled beneath her feet.

The moonlight and the stars suddenly seemed a whole lot brighter, making her feel more vulnerable, more exposed. Her mouth was dry as sandpaper. Shit. She'd made a huge mistake. Kayleigh was right. She shouldn't have followed this group. She should at least have been more careful. Because two against five wasn't too bad when the five weren't aware of you... but when they were, it was a different story entirely.

She stood there. Heart racing. She didn't know what to do. Didn't know where to hide. Felt like there was no place to go.

She knew she had to get away.

Because those insurgents were looking right at her.

She couldn't hold back any longer.

She turned. Ran. Ran with Kayleigh by her side, back towards the caravans.

She swore she heard shouting. Swore she heard footsteps. Swore she heard so much... but at the same time, she had no clue at all if she was just imagining it all.

Just had to keep going.

Just had to run.

She ran. Almost stumbled. *Watch yourself. Be fucking careful.*

She looked over her shoulder.

Movement.

Movement racing towards her.

"Shit."

She kept on going as those footsteps closed in, and she ran until she saw the caravans. Threw herself underneath one of them. It was the only thing she could think to do.

Kayleigh followed her closely.

She dragged herself under the caravan. Cobwebs clung to her face. Woodlice crawled over her body. In the corner of the darkness, rats scurried around excitedly.

She lay there on her front and held on to her rifle. She had to be ready. Had to be completely ready to fire at all times.

She had to wait for them, and then she had to do what had to be done.

She had no idea how long she'd been waiting, holding her breath, when the figures appeared right ahead of her.

She watched them walk around. Watched them traipse from side to side. Heard them chatting. Bickering. Arguing.

She saw them walking around so close, and she thought about firing at them. Putting bullets into their legs. She could do it right now. She had the capability. She had the position. In a weird kind of way, she had the upper hand.

And she had the anger, too. That anger burning through her. That sense that an injustice had been done and that she had to set the record straight.

She watched those feet and legs pass by and tightened her grip on the trigger when suddenly, she saw them take off in another direction, all of them. Like they'd heard something. Been distracted by something.

She loosened her grip on the trigger. Lay there. Heart pounding so hard against the ground she could feel herself bouncing. They were gone. And the weird thing about it? A part of her felt disappointed that she hadn't been able to kill them.

When she was absolutely sure they were gone, she dragged herself from under the caravan immediately.

"Hey," Kayleigh said.

But Aoife wasn't in the mood for listening to her.

Kayleigh yanked her back, pushed her, stopped her going any further. "Hey. What the fuck do you think you're doing?"

"I'm trying to find them before we lose them. So we can follow them."

"You almost got us killed right now. And we know where their home is. We've done enough. It's time to fall back."

But Aoife could only shake her head. She couldn't agree. She'd seen these people, and they were so close. There were only five of them. And that guy, Vernon. The way he'd spoken about their people. Spoken about their dead. She couldn't let that guy just walk away.

"I'm going after them," Aoife said. "You should head back. Give Harvey a heads up where I'm going."

"I can't believe you," Kayleigh said. "I can't *actually* believe you."

"Well, you'd better start doing. Head back. I'll follow them. Probably safer just one of us anyway."

She didn't even look at Kayleigh when she turned around this time.

But it didn't take her long for her to hear those footsteps getting closer.

She stopped. Felt her shoulders slumping. "I thought you were heading back?"

"I'm not leaving you on your own out here."

"I can handle myself."

"I'm not leaving you on your own, Aoife, because I…"

"Because you what?"

She saw the way Kayleigh looked into her eyes. And she felt it.

She felt like she knew what Kayleigh was going to say already, even though she hadn't said it. She'd felt that tension before. That unspoken tension. She'd buried her head in the sand. Denied things. Resisted things. Because it made things too complicated. Muddied the waters too much.

But right now, she knew exactly what Kayleigh was about to say.

She just couldn't face it.

"You should head back," Aoife said, cheeks burning. "Really. That's the safest choice right now."

"We should *both* head back. *That's* the safest choice. But sometimes we don't do the right fucking thing, do we?"

Aoife nodded. "Fair enough. So are you in?"

Kayleigh shook her head. Sighed. And then she shrugged her shoulders. "Looks like I'm always in, doesn't it?"

They took off, the pair of them. Headed off in the direction of the footprints and the general direction of Liskeard. Quite a way away, so they'd be walking a while. Shame the power at Sanctuary hadn't quite extended to a good fleet of cars just yet. Mad, really. Had helicopters, had all the technology and capabilities they had but hadn't quite got round to cars.

But as she walked, the whole time, Aoife got the feeling there was someone close.

Someone watching.

They reached the end of the footprints, and Aoife's stomach sank.

"We've lost them," Aoife said. "All this way, and we've frigging lost them."

"I know you don't want to hear it. But maybe it really is time we started talking about heading back now."

Aoife didn't want to accept it, didn't want to hear it, but she couldn't resist it anymore. Kayleigh was right.

They knew enough. And they'd gone far enough.

It was time to head back.

She went to turn around when she saw something, right in the distance.

She looked around at it.

"Aoife?" Kayleigh said.

"Ssh."

"What—"

"Ssh."

She crouched down. Crept alongside the path. Through towards the trees.

And when she saw what was down the hill, her heart started racing harder, and a smile crept up her face.

People.

Fires burning.

Some kind of camp.

"They're here," Aoife said. "This is their home."

CHAPTER FIFTEEN

Aoife stared down the slope towards the community and could barely contain her excitement—or her nerves.

It was pitch black, but there was a warm light to this place. Flame lit torches casting an amber glow, cutting through the darkness. The smell of smoke. And of food, too. Burned meat, making Aoife salivate. There were a few tents scattered around, all in pretty shitty condition. It didn't look like this place was well-equipped, that was for sure.

Certainly didn't look like the hideout of any kind of well-oiled operation.

A couple of people were about, but they didn't look armed. And they looked thin. Weak. Tribal, almost.

And it bothered Aoife even more that this group had been able to get so close to their walls. That they'd been able to launch an attack on the scale they had.

If they'd been dealt with sooner, they could have been well and truly crushed.

She felt herself shaking. Thought of Gregg. Thought of him lying there, that lifeless gaze. She thought of the screams. Of the panic. Of the confusion. Of the trauma that split through their perfect home, so cruelly. So unexpectedly. Against all logic and against all order. Against everything she'd thought possible because she buried her head so deeply in the sand and told herself it couldn't be that way. That their world was perfect, and it was unwavering, and that things were never going to change.

She saw this community right before her, and she felt herself swell with anger.

She went to throw herself down the slope towards the community, rifle in hand, when she felt a hand tighten around her arm.

She looked around. Saw Kayleigh staring at her, shaking her head.

"You aren't going to try and stop me again, are you?" Aoife asked.

"You know we can't just go charging down there."

"There's barely any of them," Aoife said. "And the ones that are there hardly look well-armed."

"They staged an attack on Sanctuary, Aoife," Kayleigh said. "A frigging devastating attack. You really think there's just a few of them? That this is head of operations, or whatever?"

Aoife heard what Kayleigh was saying. She really did. She got her logic. This did seem odd. Something didn't feel right about it at all.

And yet...

"I don't care who they are. Whether they're head of operations or just foot soldiers. You heard what they said. They're a part of the insurgent group. They're terrorists. And they're the people who killed our people."

"But Harvey said—"

"I know exactly what Harvey said," Aoife said.

"We got away with it once before. Barely made it out alive. If... if we're going to do this, let's at least assess things a little. Let's at least figure out what the hell's going on. How many of them there are. Any weaknesses, anything like that. Let's... let's just take a breath here. No 'ignorance is bliss' bullshit here. We can't afford that."

It irked Aoife, hearing Kayleigh speak to her like that. She knew she was getting at her with that "ignorance is bliss" jibe. It was clearly directed at her. Something she outright rejected. But fuck. Now wasn't the time to be debating shit like that.

She stared down the muddy slope, still in a slippery condition after the storm. Down towards that little camp. Saw the two of them sitting there, the guy with the bald head. The woman who looked practically asleep.

They could go in there.

They could take them both out.

They could begin making them pay...

No. Not making them pay. Because this wasn't about revenge. This was about justice. This was about protecting Sanctuary from more waves of attacks from these people.

Because they were bitter, and they were jealous, and they were never going to stop.

"We need to drop back," Kayleigh said. "We need to see what we're dealing with. Or we're going to get ourselves killed."

Aoife nodded. She knew Kayleigh was right.

And then she heard the man speak.

"Where the others at, Shannon?" he said. "Not keen on spending tonight guarding this place with just you."

It was that which did it for Aoife. That which changed every-thing. That which tipped the scales.

These two were on their own.

They were guarding this place on their own.

Which meant they were sitting ducks.

She looked at Kayleigh. Saw how she stared back at her, eyes wide like even she couldn't defend herself anymore. Like there was only one option here now.

"You know what we have to do," Aoife said. "While it's just the two of them. While we have a chance."

Kayleigh opened her mouth. Then she closed it. Shook her head. "It doesn't matter what I say. You've already made your mind up."

"Good," Aoife said. "You're learning."

She turned around, then. Looked at the people sitting there, right in the middle of this shitty camp.

"Come on," she said. "Let's get started."

And then she climbed down the slope towards the camp.

CHAPTER SIXTEEN

Yuri held his breath as the two women bickered amongst themselves just outside the camp, and he prayed this worked out how he wanted it to.

He couldn't hear them properly. But even then, they were arguing far louder than they thought they were, clearly. And Yuri could tell from the tension between them they were debating exactly what he wanted them to debate.

He just hoped the person he *wanted* to win the debate reigned victorious in the end.

He had a quiet confidence that would be the case. She didn't seem the kind of woman to back down.

And that would be her downfall.

He saw the skinnier woman lower her head. Shake it.

And then he saw them begin to turn around.

And at that moment, he braced himself for defeat. He braced himself for this plan not to go as expected. Always a possibility, of course, but not the way he hoped it would go.

And then he heard his people speak.

Heard Vernon. "Where the others at, Shannon? Not keen on spending tonight guarding this place with just you."

He heard those words from Vernon's mouth, and he wanted to hug the man. He was a genius. He knew exactly why he'd said what he'd said. His timing was perfect. Impeccable.

And if he was right, if his instincts were correct, it might just tip the scales in his favour all over again.

He saw the women turn around.

Saw the dark-haired woman look back at the other one.

Saw that the dynamic had shifted once more in an instant.

And then he saw them begin to descend the slope.

Guns in hand.

Towards the camp.

Yuri took a deep breath, and he smiled.

Vernon, you absolute genius.

He tightened his grip around his rifle.

Behind, he heard the rest of his people shuffling with nerves, with excitement.

So many of them, standing right behind him, waiting for their moment.

"Come on," he said. "It's time."

They watched the women descend the slope.

And then, they stepped out of the darkness.

CHAPTER SEVENTEEN

Aoife walked down the slope towards the camp with Kayleigh, and she couldn't shake the horrible feeling something was wrong.

She kept her eyes on the people in the middle of the camp. Stared right at them. She didn't want to let them out of her sight, even though they were already really close as it was. She looked around a couple of times, scanning her surroundings. She didn't see anything but empty tents. Old, burned-out fires, which looked like they'd last been lit long ago. By all accounts, this place was empty. Abandoned. It wasn't an outpost that was regularly well guarded or attended.

But someone was coming here. People were coming here.

Aoife didn't know when or where from, only that they were.

And that meant she had to get to these two guarding the place —quickly.

She thought about what she was going to do to them. How she was going to handle them. Her initial gut instinct was to take them out, one by one. Don't even give them a chance to argue their case or give them the chance to defend themselves. They didn't deserve that much. They'd given up that privilege when they'd attacked Sanctuary. When they'd killed Gregg and so many others.

But on the other hand... there was another option. Another choice. A better choice. These people could be useful. They were insurgents. Which meant they'd have information. Information on the rest of the insurgents. Information on the attack.

And they could point them to their leader.

She saw the man staring up into space. Vernon, she thought she'd heard him called. The woman, Shannon, beside him, similarly distant. They were both within shooting distance. So close Aoife could take them both out in an instant.

But she had to keep it cool. Had to keep it calm. She couldn't risk jeopardising any of this. Not after coming so far. Kayleigh was right. They'd taken enough risks as it was. Didn't want to go taking any more.

"Something's not right," Kayleigh said.

Aoife felt the hairs on the back of her neck stand on end when Kayleigh said those words. Because she felt it too. Something didn't feel right. Something didn't feel right at all.

She just didn't want to accept that might be the case.

She looked around. Looked at the empty tents. Looked at the old, burned-out fires. She looked at the traces that people had lived here. So many traces of poverty. So many signs that these people had been living in shitty conditions.

And it made sense. Made sense why they would be envious of Sanctuary. Of why they'd be so bitter about Aoife's home.

But then... why had that bitterness crossed over into violence?

What kind of monsters did the things they'd done—to innocent people?

Aoife took a deep breath. Now wasn't the time to debate morality.

Now was the time for action.

She turned towards the man again and tightened her grip on the rifle.

It all happened so fast.

The man stood.

He stood, and he turned around, and so too did the woman.

And just like that, out of nowhere, the pair of them took off and disappeared into the darkness.

Aoife froze. Kayleigh was still, right beside her. Both stood there on this slope, and suddenly Aoife felt very out in the open. She felt very exposed.

"Where the hell did they go?" Kayleigh asked.

Aoife's heart raced. She didn't want to entertain the possibility that she'd lost them. That they'd done a runner. Maybe they'd seen her. Maybe they'd seen them both, and they were getting into position, and they were going to launch an attack.

Or maybe there was a simpler explanation. A more innocent explanation.

She didn't know. She didn't have a clue. Her heart raced, and her head span.

She had no idea only that she had to get to them. She had to find them. She couldn't let them escape. She couldn't let them get away.

She started walking faster. Walking towards the darkness into which they'd disappeared. And she swore she heard things, this time. She swore she heard voices. Whispers. When she turned around, looked up into the trees, she swore she saw movement. Shadows.

No. It's all in your mind. All in your goddamned head. Keep it grounded. Don't lose your shit. Don't lose it. Not now.

"Aoife," Kayleigh said. "We need to get out of here. We need to go. Something's not right at all."

Aoife heard Kayleigh. As always, she heard her loud and clear.

But there was that rival voice. That rival force pulling her in the other direction. That rival voice whispering at her, screaming into her mind.

That image of Gregg's face.

Of his vacant eyes.

Of the smell of blood.

The sound of screams.

And that deep sense of injustice, right at the pit of her stomach.

"We can't let them get away," Aoife said. "We can't just let them go."

"Aoife—"

But Aoife wasn't listening anymore.

She ran around the back of the tents, right where the duo had disappeared.

She held her rifle, ready to fire at anything that moved.

She stepped around the back and went to pull the trigger when suddenly she froze.

Suddenly, everything stood still.

Because standing right there before her, she saw something she didn't expect to see.

A child.

A young kid. No older than five. A girl, by the looks of things. Dirty. Snotty. Bloodshot eyes as she stared right up at Aoife, right into her eyes, confused.

Afraid.

"What..." Aoife started.

And then she saw more of them.

More kids, just like this one. Men and women, too.

Except these ones weren't looking at her with confusion.

Some of them were looking at her with hatred.

That's when she heard Kayleigh.

"Aoife!"

Aoife turned around.

Ran away from the people, as much as it didn't make sense, as much as she wanted to understand.

She couldn't leave Kayleigh back there, wherever she was, whatever she'd got herself into.

She stepped back around the front of the tents, and her stomach sank.

People were approaching from the woods by the side of the camp.

Lots of people.

A hell of a lot of them. More than Aoife could count.

But as she stood there, shaking, one thing was for sure.

This was a trap.

This was a trap, and she'd walked right into it.

CHAPTER EIGHTEEN

Aoife looked all around and realised she and Kayleigh were completely surrounded.

Torchlights engulfed her. Everywhere Aoife looked, she saw someone. Insurgents holding knives and guns and coming towards her.

Another thing that struck Aoife was just how filthy they all looked. Just how malnourished and pale they all looked. Scarily so. They looked like typical post-apocalyptic villains. The sorts of people she wouldn't be surprised to learn going full cannibal, or something like that.

And yet... there was something that Aoife couldn't shift from her mind.

That child.

The child standing behind the tent. The girl who'd stood there, innocent little look on her pale face.

Staring up at her with wide, wondrous eyes.

And then the rest of them.

The children, and the other people, right behind her.

Like they were hiding.

Who were they? Prisoners? Captives?

Something told her that wasn't exactly correct, and yet she wasn't even sure why.

She'd come so close to shooting her. To pulling the trigger. She'd committed to firing at anything that moved.

But those kids...

They weren't what she expected to come across in this place.

Not what she expected to come across at all.

She looked around and held her rifle close, but she knew it was no use now.

She was surrounded.

They were both surrounded.

They'd walked right into a trap.

And that was on her.

She listened to the footsteps hit the ground. She heard the chattering. The whispering amongst one another. She saw those eyes staring at her. Staring at Kayleigh. Like *they* were the insurgents. Like they were the enemy. Like they were filth.

She saw them all surrounding her. Her heart raced. Her mouth was dry. She could smell body odour. A reminder of how she'd smelled until being fortunate enough to find herself in Sanctuary.

Only she was nothing like these people.

These monsters.

She looked at them all, and she tried to seek out an escape route. Tried to find a way she could sneak between them and get the hell away from these people.

But the more she looked, the more she realised it was no use.

She was fucked.

They were both fucked.

She looked closer at these people. Men. Women. All of them staring at Kayleigh, who stood right beside her. None of them saying a word. Like they were waiting for Aoife or Kayleigh to break the silence.

And then, out of nowhere, a man stepped forward and walked to the front of the group.

He was tall. Bearded. Dark hair, deep brown eyes. Real serious look on his face. He looked healthier than the rest of the people here, somehow. Better built. A real sense of authority about him, right from the off.

The bloke didn't have to introduce himself for Aoife to know right away he was the leader of this group.

The leader of the insurgents.

Hate filled her veins. A lust for revenge that she hadn't felt so strongly for so, so long. Not since Grace.

She had to breathe through that. Remind herself it wasn't healthy. And it wasn't why she was here.

"For all your organisation," the man said, "you're more foolish than you look for walking right into a trap like this."

So there it was. Shit. Confirmation, not that Aoife needed it. Salt in the fucking wound. They'd walked right into a trap. Been blinded by the fact that there were two people here, and gone wandering right in. Kayleigh was right. They should have held back. They should have been more careful. Shown more caution. She'd let emotion get in the way, and it had got them caught up in a shitstorm.

She looked over at Kayleigh. Saw her glaring at her. Knew she was in deep shit with her—if ever they got out of this mess. Aoife had taken the lead. Kayleigh hadn't wanted to. It was on her. Completely on her. And she had to own her mistake.

"You killed our people," Aoife said, speaking up. Because what other choice did she have? "You slaughtered them."

Gasps amongst the crowd. Heads shaking.

The man—the leader—kept his composure. Narrowed his eyes. "Is that what they tell you? Are those the stories you tell yourselves to help you sleep at night?"

Aoife tried to step forward, instantly felt hands tightening, pulling her back. Someone holding her back. Stopping her progressing. "It's not a story. I watched people die. People I care about have died. All because, what? Because you're jealous of what we've got? Because you can't stand that we've got power and you don't?"

Again, more gasps. People shaking their heads, muttering amongst one another.

And the leader of the group holding his ground. Staring right at her, now.

"You really believe what you're saying," he said. "Don't you?"

Aoife felt butterflies in her stomach. What the hell was he talking about? "What's there not to believe? I've seen what you people have done. I've seen it with my own eyes."

"Really? You've really seen it with your own eyes? Are you absolutely sure about that?"

Aoife went to speak. Then she realised something. Sure, she'd seen conflict. She'd seen violence between the two sides.

But had she really witnessed the attack in the way she told herself she'd seen it?

All she'd seen was an explosion.

But then...

There was no other explanation.

Right?

"Anyway," he said. "It doesn't matter. You people have already made your minds up. You're lost causes, the lot of you. When you refuse to see the truth right before your eyes... it's already too late."

Aoife could only think of one thing.

At this moment where guns were pointed at her, a moment where her life felt like it could end at any second, she could only think of one thing.

That child.

Those children.

What it meant.

The significance of it.

Nobody said anything about children.

Harvey never said anything about children.

The guns raised.

The knives raised.

Pointed at her.

Pointed at Kayleigh.

"Any last words?" the man asked.

Aoife looked right at him.

Opened her mouth.

But all she could think of was that child.

And what the man said.

You've really seen it with your own eyes? Are you absolutely sure about that?

"What hasn't Harvey told us about you?"

The man narrowed his eyes. Studied her closely, just for a second.

"What's the truth?" Aoife asked. Not even sure what she was saying or why she was saying it.

The man stared at her even closer, his eyes bloodshot, his jaw quite visibly tensing.

And that's when Aoife heard the rattle of gunfire.

CHAPTER NINETEEN

Out of nowhere, Aoife heard gunfire.

The insurgents had opened fire. At least, that's what she thought. That's what she expected to see. Because there could be no other explanation for the eruption of gunfire. Where else could it have come from?

But as she stood there, looked ahead, she saw something very unexpected.

The insurgents were tumbling to the ground. Blood spurting from their necks and chests. Bodies hitting the earth, one after another.

They were falling. They were under attack.

Someone was helping Aoife and Kayleigh.

Someone was...

She saw them then, amidst the cries and the shouts, amidst the gunfire in return. Sanctuary. Reinforcements from Sanctuary, led by Cole. She wasn't sure how many of them. Only there was enough of them.

Enough to cause a real problem to the insurgents.

Enough to wipe out as many of them as possible.

Aoife looked around at Kayleigh, saw her ducking out of the way of the crossfire. Running over towards the tents for cover.

And she was relieved about that.

Because there was something she had to do.

She turned around, first. Swung her rifle around and cracked the unsuspecting guard across his face; slammed him down to the muddy ground.

And then she looked back towards the insurgents' leader.

Yuri, people were shouting at him. So that was his name. Yuri. He was the one who was responsible for the hell Sanctuary had been through.

She needed to take him out. He was the head of the snake. Take him out, and surely the rest would fall into disarray.

He was the leader. He was responsible for the attack on Sanctuary.

Sanctuary deserved justice.

She ran ahead, over the muddy ground, over towards that crowd of insurgents. They were shooting. Fighting back. Some of them dispersing. She saw some of them running away with fear on their faces. Some of them standing their ground and firing back, even though they were on the floor, wounded, bleeding out.

She saw the whole scene, and she couldn't get that kid out of her mind.

The kid behind the tent...

She looked up and saw Yuri running off into the woods.

She gritted her teeth. She wasn't letting him go. Wasn't letting that murderous bastard weasel his way out of this one.

He was going to pay for what he'd done.

She ran up the slope towards the trees. Bullets whizzed past her, crossfire from both parties. All around her, she heard shouting. Cries. Screaming. And for a moment, just for a split second, it struck Aoife just how similar this felt to the attack at Sanctuary. To the panic and confusion she'd experienced so, so recently.

The people of this insurgent camp seemed just as terrified. And just as shocked.

And then she saw Yuri lifting a rifle and firing at her people.

She pulled her gun back, lifted it, pointed it at him. Her hands were shaky, and he was out of range, but she had a clear shot at him. A clear chance to take him out.

And then he ducked. Disappeared off, further into the woods. More of his people following him now.

She went to run after him. Up the slope. As much as she knew she should be standing alongside her people and helping, she just couldn't let Yuri get away. That would be more help in the long run. She couldn't just let him escape.

She ran further towards the trees, rifle in hand, closer to his fleeing people while the rest of them fired and fled all around, when suddenly she heard a familiar shout.

She turned around. Looked back down the slope, down towards the tents.

Kayleigh was lying on her back.

An insurgent stood over her. Pistol in hand.

Aoife froze. Dread filled her body.

Somebody was going to die.

Somebody was going to die because of *her*.

She'd walked away from Kayleigh, and now she was in danger...

She didn't even hesitate.

She lifted her rifle with her shaking hand.

Pointed at that man.

He tightened the trigger, all of it happening in slow motion.

And Aoife focused and fired.

The bullet whizzed past him.

Hit the ground beside him.

The man lowered his rifle.

Turned around.

Looked up at the trees.

And for a split second, he looked right into Aoife's eyes.

"Won't miss this time," Aoife said.

She pulled the trigger.

The man's head jolted back, and he fell to the ground right beside Kayleigh.

Aoife lowered her rifle. Looked around. The gunfire had eased now. The bulk of the insurgents—those who were still standing—had disappeared into the woods. The worst of the attack was over.

She looked around into the trees, into the darkness, over to where Yuri and the rest of his people had disappeared to. And as much as she wanted to go after him, she knew it was a fool's errand right now.

There were more of them than she could handle.

And as much as instinct told her to go after them, never to give up, she knew she didn't have a choice if she wanted to survive.

She lowered her rifle. Sighed. And she climbed back down the slope, down towards Kayleigh.

She held out a hand to help her to her feet.

Kayleigh batted it aside, and got up herself, then nudged past Aoife.

"This didn't have to happen," Kayleigh said. "None of this had to happen."

And as she walked off, the guilt growing inside Aoife, she looked over at those tents where she'd seen those children, and something in her began to wonder if everything really was as it seemed here...

____

CHAPTER TWENTY

____

Aoife and Kayleigh had no choice but to head back home in the dark with the rest of their friends from Sanctuary.

But Aoife couldn't shake the feeling that Yuri had got away with murder—and she'd been the one to let him slip away.

It was dark and cold, and to be quite honest, Aoife wasn't all that keen on talking to Kayleigh. Because she felt guilty as fuck, in all truth. Why wouldn't she? She'd dragged Kayleigh on in there, against her better judgement—and against Kayleigh's will, in a sense. She'd almost got Kayleigh killed. And a few of the reinforcements from Sanctuary had been injured and killed bailing them out of the mess they'd got themselves into.

So yeah. She couldn't help feeling a bit shitty about things right now. And she certainly didn't need Kayleigh banging on about it to remind her just how shitty she should be feeling.

But she knew Kayleigh wasn't one to hold back on how she was feeling. Especially not when she was pissed off. At least, not for long, anyway.

"You're a fucking dick for what you did," Kayleigh said.

Ah. There it was. Right on cue, right as Aoife expected. She supposed she couldn't really complain or argue, though. She *had* been a dick. As much as she'd told herself she was doing what was right... she felt guilty. Rightly so.

"Kayleigh—"

"I don't want to hear any crap about how sorry you are or how you thought you were doing the right thing. I don't want to hear any of that, Aoife. You got us in the shit. Deep, deep shit. You almost got yourself killed, and you almost got me killed. You ended up pissing those terrorists off and got a bunch of our people hurt and killed. I know, I know, they say they came in to fight for justice anyway, whatever. But even so. We could've done things differently. We had an advantage, and we blew it. You blew it."

Aoife didn't know what to say as she walked in the darkness with Kayleigh. They weren't far from home, so she figured she'd just have to take her grilling. She deserved it. Couldn't exactly complain.

"You're blinkered, and you're ignorant, and you're selfish, and you always have been."

Ouch. That one stung a little. Just keep walking. Just keep calm. Don't react...

"No wonder you've got people killed in the fucking past."

"Hey," Aoife said.

She turned on Kayleigh then. Because that comment, that was crossing the line.

But she could see the look in Kayleigh's eyes. She could see she was out of control. That she was on the verge of saying *anything*—and that she didn't have any regrets.

That she was just daring herself to say something else. To push Aoife some more.

"Anything else?" Aoife said. "Anything else you want to get off your chest while we're here?"

Kayleigh opened her mouth. Like she was really thinking about it.

And then she closed it. Shook her head. "There's nothing I need to say. You torture yourself about shit enough."

She walked off ahead of Aoife, then. And something about it bugged Aoife more than anything. The way she'd looked at her— looked *down* at her...

"Fuck this," Aoife said.

She marched off after Kayleigh. She wasn't letting her have the last word in this one. Definitely wasn't going to be made to feel like the bad one for sticking up for her community, for trying to do something for her home.

"Sanctuary came under attack," Aoife said. "People died. Gregg died. So many people died."

"I know that," Kayleigh said. "I live there too. You're not the only one who's lost people."

"Harvey sent us out to get intel. We had a chance—"

"We walked right into a trap," Kayleigh said. "A trap I saw coming miles away. And don't say I could have walked away or some shit like that. You're my friend. And friends don't walk away."

She wanted to say something else, wanted to keep this fight going, wanted to keep on arguing her ground and standing up for herself.

But she knew there was nothing else she could say.

"Let's just get back home," Kayleigh said. "Today's done. We go home. We reflect. And... and whatever happens next, happens."

Aoife nodded. She figured that was the best approach right now. Just get the hell back home, then figure out their next step.

"I saw children," Aoife said.

Kayleigh frowned. "Huh?"

"Behind the tents. I saw... I saw kids. They looked... I don't know. But they didn't look like..."

Kayleigh didn't say anything. Just stared at her. Shook her

head. "Stands to reason a group that big are gonna have kids around. What did you expect?"

Aoife wasn't sure what she expected. Kayleigh had a point.

But just seeing those children. Seeing the innocent, scared looks on their faces...

She realised she'd been telling herself the insurgents were something other than human for a while now. Everyone had been treating them like phantoms rather than people.

Seeing them, being in their camp...

Something felt different.

"Come on," Kayleigh said. "Let's get back. I want some sleep before light. Can't sleep for shit in the light."

Aoife nodded. Looked back into the woods.

Then she took a deep breath and walked off after Kayleigh.

They walked in silence until they saw Sanctuary in the distance.

Aoife felt a warmth. Always nice seeing home. For more than a moment earlier, she'd felt that she might never see it again.

"I appreciate what you were trying to do," Kayleigh said. "Just... pull your head out of the sand sometimes. The world's a whole lot bigger than you think it is. Things aren't always so black and white."

She didn't know what Kayleigh meant by that. Or at least what its relevance was to everything that'd happened.

But before she could ask her about it, she heard rustling in the trees.

She looked back. Saw Cole and the other Sanctuary friends who'd come to her aid.

And then behind them, she saw insurgents jumping out.

"Cole!" Aoife shouted.

But it was already too late.

The insurgents buried their blades into the throats of their friends.

Of their colleagues.

Of Cole.

Aoife's stomach sank.

Fear engulfed her.

She watched as they flooded out of the trees, as Cole clutched his throat and fell to the forest floor.

He was dead.

They'd fucking killed him.

She went to lift her rifle with her shaking hands and fire at them when she heard movement behind her.

The next thing she knew, she felt a crack on the head, and darkness.

CHAPTER TWENTY-ONE

Aoife opened her eyes.

It was dark. Pitch black all around her. For a moment, she felt totally calm. That feeling you get when you wake up and you've almost forgotten your problems. Your responsibilities. Your entire sense of self.

But then a niggling doubt crept in. Butterflies in her stomach.

Something was wrong.

Very wrong.

The air in the room was cool. Far cooler than her bedroom at home at Sanctuary. It was quiet, too. Totally quiet. Sanctuary was never truly quiet. Because of the electricity. Never underestimate the power of... well, *power*. You only realise its radiant noise when you've lost it. Far noisier than anyone ever gives it credit for.

But in here, nothingness. An emptiness. It was unfamiliar. Alienating.

And there was the taste of blood in the back of her throat, too.

She didn't notice it at first. But now, it was strong. Metallic. And her head ached like mad, too.

Something had happened. Something at the insurgent camp. Something with that man, Yuri...

Only... no. That's not how it'd gone down.

They'd got away from that place. She, Kayleigh, and those who came to their rescue, too. They'd got away. They were so close to home, and then...

She remembered.

Insurgents emerging from the woods.

Stabbing her people.

Stabbing Cole.

Turning around with her rifle, fear paralysing her.

And then feeling something smack her on the head, total darkness, and then...

Well. This.

She tried to turn around. She was gagged. Sitting upright from the feel of it, too. In some uncomfortable-as-fuck chair, forcing her spine totally erect.

Her wrists were tied behind the back of the chair. Ankles, too. Not an unfamiliar position to be in. She'd been captured and trapped a bunch of times since the power went out. It was almost becoming routine at this point.

But it never got any less scary. After all, she knew she wasn't meant to make it out of situations like this. Nobody captured someone like this and intended them to escape.

But she had to. Her life depended on it.

She thought of Kayleigh, and her stomach sank. She didn't know what'd happened to her. Whether she'd met the same fate as the other people she'd watched die. She wanted to shout out for her in some slim hope that she might be close by, but she knew it was useless. And she was gagged anyway, so what good would it be?

She pulled her wrists apart, hard as she could. Then tried her ankles. No luck with either of them. The darkness was getting more and more intense; more and more intimidating. She knew she needed to get out of here. For whatever reason, they'd kept her alive.

She hoped to God they hadn't kept her alive for the same reason as so many despicable men kept women alive in times of conflict...

The thought of it made her want to vomit.

She pulled even harder at the ties around her wrists, but no luck. The more she pulled, the more she wondered if they were solid handcuffs wrapped around her. Which meant she was in an even shittier mess than she'd first imagined.

She tried yanking her ankles apart again, hope dwindling at this point.

But then she felt something.

The ankle ties. They weren't as solid as the wrist ones. They felt looser somehow.

She yanked at them again, tried to pull them apart.

And she realised whatever was around them was loosening.

Rope.

Only loosely tied, too.

She sat there a few seconds, almost in disbelief. It seemed bizarre they'd go to the lengths of tying her up in here only to fail to tie her ankles properly.

But she couldn't get caught up in that shit.

At the end of the day, she couldn't overthink things. She just had to get the hell out of here.

She pulled at the ties even more. Pulled harder and harder, until eventually, they just fell away.

And then she stood up.

Dragged her handcuffed arms from behind the chair.

Tried to shake free of her blindfold, but no use.

She crouched down. Pulled at her blindfold against the edge of the chair. Heart racing. Hope rising.

She was getting out of this.

She was finding Kayleigh, and she was getting the hell away from this place.

She dragged the blindfold against the chair, trying and trying, desperate to just see so she could be less disoriented, so she knew exactly where she was.

She kept on trying, but the blindfold was tight, hard to shake free.

She heard footsteps outside.

Someone approaching.

She had to be fast.

She had to think quick.

She had to get out while she could.

She dragged the blindfold against the side of the chair again when it fell back.

Darkness.

Only not as dark as the one she'd been plugged into behind the blindfold.

She could see.

She looked around the room. Dark. Empty. Grey. Dismal. Just that one chair, right in the middle. Looked like she was in some kind of emptied-out, dusty old garage.

She went to turn around and figure out her best way out of here when she saw someone standing there in the darkness.

Someone familiar.

Serious expression on his big, bearded face.

"I don't think so," Yuri said.

CHAPTER TWENTY-TWO

Aoife saw Yuri standing opposite her, and immediately her stomach sank.

It'd been a trick. The whole fucking thing had been a trick. He'd been standing there the whole time. Watching her struggle. Watching her trying to break out.

And why?

She didn't know why. Only that she saw the way he was looking at her. Staring at her. That serious look on his face. A serious look that never shifted.

"I'm sorry for how you ended up here. But you didn't really expect me to just let you go after what happened, did you?"

Aoife couldn't speak. She was still gagged. Her wrists were still tied behind her back. But she could see now, and her feet were free, so that was something at least.

She looked around the room for a way out. A chance to dart. A chance to break free.

"The door's locked behind me," Yuri said. "You can look all you want. Have a wander if you fancy. If it'll make you feel better. But trust me. You might as well save your energy 'cause there's no way out of this place."

Aoife wanted to look anyway. Wanted to search every inch of this room. She'd got out of shittier situations before.

Or maybe she hadn't. Maybe this was the one she was finally going to find herself trapped in, once and for all.

She stood there with her gag around her mouth and stared at Yuri as he stood with his hands behind his back, peering at her in the darkness.

He walked towards her slowly. "For someone who knows exactly what they're responsible for, you're looking awfully confused about why you're here."

Knows what she's responsible for? What the hell was he talking about? Sure, those Sanctuary reinforcements had come in and murdered a bunch of his people. But if it weren't for the attacks from the insurgents in the first place, that shit would never have happened. They could have lived in peace.

"But you know," Yuri said, walking closer to her, "I've started to think. To really, really think about something you said yesterday when we captured you."

Yesterday? Shit. Had she really been out that long?

He walked right up to her. So close to her now. She could smell the sweat and slight sourness to his breath. Only this time, as he looked her in the eye, she saw a glint of something she hadn't seen before. Was it a tear? A trickle of emotion?

He reached up and grabbed the side of her head, and for a moment, she thought he might just slam her skull against the solid floor.

But he didn't.

He pulled her gag away.

She coughed. Coughed so much she heaved, then vomited bloody bile, crouching there on her knees.

But she didn't want to stay down. Didn't want to portray any sort of weakness to this monster.

She looked up at him. Shaking. "You have some fucking nerve."

He smiled. For the first time, he actually smiled. "*I* have some nerve? You're the one with nerve. Creeping on into our camp. Having my people surrounded and slaughtered. Then having the audacity to look me in the eye like I'm the one with the problem?"

"None of this would've happened if you hadn't attacked our people. If you hadn't terrorised us for God knows how long."

Yuri stopped walking towards Aoife. He shook his head, staring at her blankly. "You really don't know, do you?"

"I know all I need to know about you."

Yuri looked in his own world. "At first, I thought you were bluffing. I wasn't sure. I thought about killing you, just like we always kill you. But now I see... you're being sincere, aren't you? You really don't know?"

"I know you killed my friends. I know you're a bunch of selfish, bitter people who can't bear the fact that we have what you don't. And I know I'm going to make you pay for what you've done."

"All this time and I've had it wrong," Yuri said. "Totally wrong."

"What the fuck are you blabbing on about?"

He looked back at the door. Again, like he was in a world of his own. Then he looked back at her. "I don't know how to say this. And I know you're not going to like what I have to say. But I have to start somewhere. Somebody has to start somewhere."

"You can start by telling me my friend's okay. That Kayleigh's okay."

"Oh, Kayleigh," Yuri said. "Kayleigh is just fine. Don't worry. We're taking good care of her."

Aoife didn't like his tone, the way he said that. She launched up. Walked over to him. Squared right up to him. "I might be cuffed. But I'll find a way to get to you. I don't need my hands to make you suffer."

He searched her eyes closely. That flat expression to his face once more. Then he took a deep breath through his nose, sighed. "Nobody's going to be fighting anybody. Not today."

He turned around. Walked over to the door. Turned a key and then opened it. A noisy rusty sound of metal on metal echoed around the damp room.

"I'm not the villain you think I am."

"Bullshit. I've seen what you are for myself."

"You keep saying you've seen things. You keep insisting I'm this, and I'm that. But you haven't, have you?"

She saw him look back at her. Saw that look in his eyes.

And then she thought of the children she'd seen.

"You talk about seeing. About how so much of your faith is in what you've supposedly seen. Well, how about you follow me and come see for yourself a different version of events?"

A chill crept up Aoife's spine. "I don't understand."

"Follow me, and you will. Or are you just too scared to see the truth?"

She stood there. Caught between two worlds. On the one hand, she wanted to stay put. She didn't want to move a muscle. Because she was afraid. Afraid of what she might see. Afraid her whole world might come tumbling down all around her.

"Join me. And you'll be able to comment on what you've *seen* then."

She took a deep breath.

Clutched her fists.

Stared at that open, dark door, right before her, right beyond Yuri.

She didn't want to move.

She didn't want to go.

But she knew she had no choice.

She took another deep breath, and she walked.

CHAPTER TWENTY-THREE

"Follow me," Yuri said.

Aoife stood at the garage door. Yuri stood ahead of her, right in front of that dark void that led back outside. She didn't want to go out there. She didn't want to see whatever it was he wanted to show her.

Because she had a bad feeling.

A bad feeling that whatever it was might fuck with her worldview.

That he had something momentous, and it was about to change her mind about everything.

She thought about the children she'd seen. The innocent people. And part of her started to wonder.

What if there was more to that than she first thought?

What if there was more to it than there seemed to be?

But... no. They were insurgents. They'd put Sanctuary through hell. It didn't matter *what* Yuri told her or what he showed her. Nothing changed that.

"Come on," he said. "Don't make me drag you out."

Aoife swallowed a lump in her dry throat.

She looked down at the concrete floor and took a deep breath.

She figured she didn't have a choice.

She walked out through the door. Her wrists still bound behind her back. As she stepped outside, she realised it was dark. The only light from the flickering flames of the fires all around this camp.

She looked around the camp. Squinted. She could see people. More people than before. This place looked different to the one she'd reached last night. They must've moved her somewhere else. It was more urban somehow, even though there were still trees around. Some kind of log cabin site, by the looks of things.

The people stared at her as she walked past, Yuri right behind her, hand on her back. She could see them whispering to one another. Shaking their heads. Looking at Aoife like she was the enemy. Like *she* should be looking at them for the things they'd done.

"Keep moving," Yuri said. "We don't have all night."

Aoife turned from the people and walked. Walked past more of those cabins. And now, she was really getting an insight into the scale of this place. The number of people here. They didn't exactly look well-armed. But there were a lot of them, and she could see how this number of people could be a force to be reckoned with.

She turned around and saw where Yuri was leading her, and her stomach sank.

The woods.

Out into the woods.

Her heart picked up.

He was going to take her out into the woods and do God knows with her.

She felt her jaw tensing, her teeth grinding against one another. She didn't know why she was so sure something bad would happen in those woods. If Yuri wanted to kill her, he'd do it right here, in front of his people.

But something just screamed at Aoife that the woods didn't mean anything good. It never did.

"Go on," Yuri said. Narrowing his eyes and staring right at her.

"Kayleigh," Aoife said. "I want to... I want to know she's okay."

"You have my word."

"And I'm supposed to just accept that? Believe that?"

"You don't really have a choice."

Aoife wanted to argue, but she figured he was right. She didn't have a choice. Wherever Kayleigh was, she had no power right now. She had no options right now.

Just walking towards those woods. Towards where Yuri wanted her to go.

She looked back at this community. At the camp the insurgents were living in.

Took a deep breath.

And then she turned around and walked towards the woods.

She hoped the sight of that insurgent camp wasn't the last thing she saw.

She kept on going for a while. Stumbling over a few times, Yuri propping her up, helping her to her feet. He didn't say much. And when she tried speaking to him, he didn't respond.

"How much further?" she asked.

Nothing.

She walked further into the woods. Deeper in. Over a stream, cold water freezing against her bare ankles. Above, the moonlight beamed down.

"If you're going to kill me, just tell me. Just... just tell me so I can at least fucking prepare myself.

"I'm not going to kill you," Yuri said. "Not yet anyway."

"Wow. Reassuring."

"Not my job to reassure you. Anyway. It's right here. Right up ahead. Then you'll finally see for yourself."

She swallowed a lump in her throat. Squinted ahead. "I don't see anything."

Yuri walked in front of her now. Walked right up to two small trees growing from the ground. Looked down at them. And looked transfixed by them. So transfixed that Aoife wondered if she might actually be able to run away.

"I don't... I don't understand."

Yuri looked over at her. And in the brightness of the beaming sun, she saw something unexpected.

There were tears in his eyes.

"What..."

It suddenly dawned on her, then.

These weren't just any old trees.

They were crosses.

Two little hand-made crosses in the ground before her.

"What... what is this place?" she asked.

Yuri sniffed. Wiped his eyes. Cleared his throat. "This... this is where I buried my boys. My Ross. My Ben. This is where I buried them after he killed them."

Aoife frowned. "I... I don't understand—"

"I had an affair with his wife, Caroline. We... we fell in love. Harvey didn't accept it. Went full psycho. Caroline and I had the boys. He had a restraining order against his name. We didn't hear anything for years. The power went out. We lost Caroline. My dear wife. And then... and then when I was walking up to Sanctuary, trying to find a home for my boys and my people, I saw him. Saw him standing there. And I knew my hopes were dead."

Aoife shook her head. She still didn't get it. Still didn't understand. "Who was standing there? Whose wife did you have an affair with?"

"Harvey," he said. "Harvey killed my boys. He killed my boys, and he told me to stay well away from Sanctuary. He did this. Don't you see? *This* is who he is."

CHAPTER TWENTY-FOUR

"I ... I don't believe you," Aoife said.

Yuri shrugged. "Believe what you want to believe. These are my sons' graves. I'm not going to dig them up just to prove myself to you. But you should know what kind of a leader you're serving. You should know that Harvey isn't the man you want him to be. And the very foundation of your home is built on a violent lie."

Aoife stood outside the garage she'd been locked up in. It was just her and Yuri here, in a nice spot just outside a small village where it looked like the insurgents were camped out right now. Right amidst a thick bunch of trees, there were two little crosses. Two little mounds of earth.

And etched onto those wooden crosses, two names.

Ross.

Ben.

Rain sprinkled down from above now. She couldn't stop staring at those graves. She tried to tell herself this couldn't be real. That the tale Yuri told had to be a lie.

Because Harvey. Harvey wasn't a monster. A child-killing monster.

He was a good man. It was because of him that she had a home. That so many people had power. Had *hope*.

"Once Harvey knew I was out there and that I was building myself an army of my own, he had to be very careful what he told his people. I should have realised that much. He painted us as terrorists. As bitter, vicious attackers. We don't want to destroy what you have. We want things to be different. Because as long as Harvey is in charge of your community... I will never rest."

She stared at those crosses. She didn't know what to say. How to react. Only that she wasn't expecting this one bit. She felt in total turmoil. Still trying to run from the truth. Still trying to hide from what was blatantly obvious, right before her eyes.

"Your people..."

"My people, what? Attacked Sanctuary? Sure, we've had shootouts in the woods."

"You attacked us. You killed our people just days ago."

"We couldn't do that if we wanted to," Yuri said. "We don't have the power. The resources. The truth is... Harvey can only maintain control if he rules with fear over me and my people. My group, which is expanding rapidly. Who eventually *will* be able to launch a bigger attack. For a long time, he ignored us and didn't make as much of a deal of us because he didn't think we could touch him. He didn't think we had anything on him. But when he realised it was me who was the head of the snake... well. He knew he had to step things up."

Aoife shook her head. It was all she could do. All this time, and Harvey had been hunting down these people? Because he was afraid of the truth coming out?

A personal grudge? That's what this came to?

Not a legitimate conflict. Not an existential threat.

But a historical personal grudge?

"You look like you don't really know what to say," Yuri said.

"I can't... This can't be true."

"And yet you talk about seeing things. With your own eyes.

Well, look. Look at my sons' graves. Look at me. Look at me and tell me if you see a charlatan and a liar or if you see someone who has lost. Who wants to bring that bloodthirsty demon down before he destroys me and my people completely. Tell me that's what you don't see."

She looked into Yuri's eyes and saw how bloodshot they were. She saw the way his face twitched. He looked like he was almost crying.

"Tell me what you see."

She looked at him. Then she looked down at the ground.

Harvey sent her out here. He trusted her. He trusted her because she was one of his biggest and most faithful servants.

He thought she'd get the job done, no questions asked.

He thought nothing would sway her.

But now it felt like her whole reality was falling apart.

"I don't know why I'm telling you this," Yuri said. "I don't know why I've kept you alive. Because you're blinkered. You're all blinkered. You follow in his footsteps in blind faith. But... I don't know. There's something different about you. Something that made me wonder, right from the first time. Maybe I'm wrong. That's not up to me, anyway. It's up to my people to decide your fate. And I can't imagine things are going to go great for you if it's left to their judgement."

She couldn't really process his words. She just thought of those kids she'd seen. Kids, hunted down by Harvey? Hunted down by her people?

They weren't terrorists. They were just fighting for their own survival.

"All I want," Yuri said, "is to be able to live in peace. All my people want is to live in peace. As long as Harvey is around, that won't be able to happen. This isn't about revenge. It's about survival. And I was going to ask if you will help me. Because I thought I saw something different in your eyes. I really did."

Aoife narrowed her eyes. "What... How do you want my help?"

"I want you to kill Harvey. I want you to take him out. That part is non-negotiable."

Aoife shook her head. "Kill him? I'm not going to... I'm not going to fucking kill him."

"Then your fate's decided," Yuri said.

He grabbed her arm, dragged her back out of the woods, back towards camp.

"Enjoy your final hours," he said. "Because I was wrong about you. And there's only one thing that will make my people happy now."

He pulled her down towards the garage door again. Stopped outside.

And in the distance, Aoife saw a platform with a noose dangling from it, and she realised right away that it was for her.

"Think very carefully about the decisions you've made," Yuri said.

And then he threw her into the garage and slammed the door shut, surrounding her in darkness.

CHAPTER TWENTY-FIVE

Aoife sat back in the dark, dusty garage and tried to wrap her head around everything she'd learned—and what she was going to do next.

It was always dark in here. Smelled like damp. But it was quiet. Aoife needed silence right now. She needed it to figure out how the hell she was going to go from here. What choice did she have? She was locked up. Locked up because Yuri still didn't totally trust her, apparently. Dick.

But then, she couldn't hold it against him.

Not if what he'd told her was true.

And why wouldn't it be true? What reason had he given her not to believe in it?

She sat there in the darkness and kept on thinking of Yuri's two boys, Ben and Ross. Losing their mother, Caroline. Searching desperately for some kind of home with their father, some kind of safe place.

Only to run into Harvey at the gates.

Harvey shooting them in a bitter rage.

And then hunting down and trying to wipe out Yuri's people completely.

She shook her head. She still couldn't accept it. Harvey seemed so friendly. He seemed so caring. Intense and passionate about his project, sure.

But he was a good man. A good man who trusted her.

You're blinkered, and you always have been...

She remembered those words, and they stung. Was it true? Had she been so dead set on believing Sanctuary was perfect and Harvey was the ideal leader that she'd actually failed to see the cracks in the flags right before her eyes?

She didn't know. She didn't know a lot anymore.

But she knew one thing.

She'd seen Yuri killing her people. Good people. He'd captured Kayleigh, and Aoife had no idea where she was. So regardless of what he said, regardless of what had happened to him and his family, he was no angel.

But then, was she? After all, she'd done some pretty horrible things over the years in acts of revenge.

She was far from perfect herself. And she knew how blinkered the search for justice could make a person.

She closed her pulsating, burning eyes. She just wanted to wake up back at Sanctuary. Wake up days ago, before all this mess. Wake up in a time when things were good. When things were perfect. When she didn't have a thing to worry about. When nobody had a thing to worry about.

And then, out of nowhere, in her mind's eye, she saw Max.

He was looking at her like he didn't recognise her. Shaking his head.

"What's your problem, old man?" she said.

But he didn't say anything to her. Just looked at her, kept on shaking his head. Like he was judging her.

"What would you have done differently?" she asked. "If you found somewhere perfect... what would you have done differently?"

He looked away, then. Faded from view.

She wanted to scream out. Wanted to cry at him to come back. Because she didn't want to be on her own right now. She needed him right now. Needed his advice. Needed his wisdom.

But he was gone. He was long gone.

She was on her own in this one.

She thought about Yuri and what he'd been through. Thought about his goals. The survival of his people.

And she thought about what he'd said about Harvey and what Harvey wanted, too.

To eliminate the insurgents for launching their attack on Sanctuary.

But then, *had* the insurgents attacked Sanctuary at all?

Or was she supposed to believe that was an inside job like he said?

She didn't know what to think or what to believe.

Only that her time was running out.

She still couldn't believe what Yuri had said. She certainly didn't trust him. So she needed to know for sure.

She knew there was only one option. She didn't know how feasible it was. She knew she was likely not getting out of this place. But she knew what she had to do, given the opportunity.

She had to confront Harvey, and she had to find out what he had to say about all this.

He deserved a chance to have his say. She couldn't go letting herself be used as a tool by Yuri and his people when she didn't know the full facts.

She took a deep breath, went to stand from the chair, when suddenly the door opened.

Yuri stood there. Someone by his side. "I thought you might want to see each other."

The woman stepped into the room. Came into view.

"Kayleigh," Aoife said.

CHAPTER TWENTY-SIX

"So," Kayleigh said.

"Yeah," Aoife said. "'So'."

"Not exactly the predicament I imagined us ending up in."

"You can say that again."

Aoife sat there in the darkness of this garage. She wasn't tied to a chair anymore, but her wrists were still bound. The door was locked. They'd checked a couple of times. No way out of this place. Stuck in here together.

And all Aoife could think about was what Yuri had said to her.

What had happened to his children. To his two sons.

The affair he'd had with Harvey's wife and the jealous grudge Harvey had sought out ever since.

How that jealous grudge had driven Harvey even to hunt down Yuri's people.

And even worse than that.

According to Yuri, it'd prompted him to detonate a bomb amongst Sanctuary, all to wage a war against Yuri.

"Something doesn't add up," Kayleigh said.

Aoife looked at her. Staring into the darkness. Clearly just as stunned by the revelations as she was. "Huh?"

"This Yuri character. I'll keep my voice down 'cause I've no doubt he'll be listening to us. But... I dunno. Something just doesn't seem right to me. Something just doesn't, like, add up. I mean, I can believe Harvey's not as clean-cut as he first seemed. But still. All this? For a fucking grudge? It sounds mad."

Aoife nodded. "Wars have been started for less."

"Yuri kept us alive. He's killed our people, so many of our people. And yet he kept us alive. Why us?"

Aoife shook her head. "Maybe he hasn't killed as many of our people as we think. Maybe it's... maybe it's us who've been the ones in the wrong all along. And they've just been fighting for their own survival. Just like he said."

"I dunno, Aoife. But one thing's for sure."

"What's that?"

"You've changed your fucking tune."

"Huh?"

"Listen to yourself. You're sucking off Harvey one second, his special little loyal princess. And then the second your bubble bursts, you sound like you're gunning for him."

Aoife looked down, shook her head. "It's not that simple. I mean... I can't accept it. I can't believe what Yuri says about Harvey is true. But I need to look him in the eye, and I need to confront him about it. Because the more I see, and the more I think about it... I dunno. It's like I've had a plaster on and suddenly it's been torn off."

Kayleigh half-smiled, nodded. "I get that. Question is, how're we going to get out of this? Harvey might be a bad egg. But Yuri doesn't seem much better when it comes to us lot."

"I've been thinking about that," Aoife said.

"And have you reached any radical solutions?"

Aoife wished she had something profound to offer. She was

never usually short of ideas. Picked a bad fucking time for her mind to go blank.

"Let's face it," Kayleigh said. "We're stuck in a war between two wrong'uns, and there's no way out."

"And that's on me," Aoife said. "Yeah, yeah. I get it."

"Hey," Kayleigh said. "Don't go taking words out of my mouth. But no. In a way... well, whatever happens, as much as I fucking hate you for dragging me in here... I'm kind of glad it did happen."

Aoife looked up at her. "Really?"

"At least now my suspicions that Harvey's actually a creepy git are confirmed. Something you've always been too oblivious to see. If it takes almost dying to prove myself right, then that's exactly what's got to happen."

Aoife smiled. She looked away. Shook her head. "If we are going to die in here, I'm glad I'm going to die with you."

"Me too," Kayleigh said. "Me too."

They were quiet a little longer, sitting there in the darkness. Aoife had no idea how long had passed. But she felt weirdly calm. Her fate was out of her hands. And at the end of the day, they were relying on the mercy of a man who harboured revenge against Harvey and against his people as an extension of him. There was no point getting worked up about it. There would be no convincing him. There was nothing else to convince him about.

The man would make his mind up, and whatever happened would happen, whether they protested or not. Just had to accept that.

"If we don't get out of this," Kayleigh said. "I kind of wanted to say something to you."

Aoife turned. Looked at her. She was staring at the floor, twiddling with her hands. She looked like she was lost in thought. "What?"

Kayleigh glanced up at her. An innocence to her eyes now.

More like the Kayleigh she used to know. Not the hardened woman she'd become.

She opened her mouth and went to say something when the door banged open.

Aoife looked around.

Saw Yuri standing there.

By his side, two guards. Armed.

"It's time," Yuri said.

Aoife's stomach turned. "Time for what?"

"Time to pay for your crimes."

CHAPTER TWENTY-SEVEN

Aoife followed Yuri out of the garage and felt pretty fucking terrified about whatever awaited ahead.

She was blindfolded now, but her cuffs had been undone. It was like they didn't want her to see where they were taking her. She could hear things as she walked. Voices. Whispers. She swore she felt stuff too. Things being thrown at her, not heavy stuff. Maybe just spit and that sort of shit. The people here didn't like her or Kayleigh. They were the enemy in their eyes. They were the Sanctuary members, and Sanctuary had been hunting down their people for God knows how long.

Aoife still couldn't believe this all boiled down to a mere grudge. That the animosity was between two men over a woman.

Classic really, wasn't it?

Perfect, safe haven at Sanctuary, and it was a frigging love triangle that threatened to end all that was good with that place, once and for all.

Aoife walked. She felt like she'd been walking forever even though it'd probably only been minutes. She felt hot and clammy. She couldn't stop thinking of Yuri's words when he'd come into that garage for her and Kayleigh.

Time to pay for your crimes.

She knew what that meant. She knew there would only be one outcome for people like her. There was only ever one outcome for people like her.

They were going to be killed. She and Kayleigh were going to be killed in a show of strength. Yuri claimed his people had been hunted and slaughtered over a prolonged period. It didn't matter what Aoife and Kayleigh said; the people here weren't going to show any sort of compassion or forgiveness.

They were going to be out for blood.

She kept on walking until suddenly she felt herself stop.

"Up the steps," the man behind her said. One of the two holding a gun. "Not much further."

Aoife's heart raced even faster. She didn't want to walk a step further. If she climbed these steps, it'd be over. The end.

"Now," the man said, pushing her a little further.

She climbed. Climbed up the steps. Felt like there were loads of them. And she was okay with that. She wanted them to last forever. She needed time to plan. To think.

But the more she walked, it dawned on her even more that there was nothing to plan. There was nothing to think about.

This only ended one way.

She felt the top of the steps, then the man turned her and walked her further along.

And then, one more turn, and she stopped.

She stood there. Hands on her shoulders. Not moving. Just still. Totally still.

And Aoife felt like time had stood still. She felt like this was a moment everything had been building towards. She almost didn't want her blindfold to be pulled away. Because she was afraid.

She held her breath, her heart racing faster and faster.

And then, suddenly, her vision returned.

It was light. That was the first thing that struck her. Made her squint. Only as she blinked, she realised there were torches lighting the air up. It wasn't day, not yet. A jet-black sky above, not a star in sight.

Ahead of her, people. Lots of people. At least fifty of them. All standing there. Many holding torches.

She saw their pale gazes. Their malnourished bodies. Men. Women. Children. These were the so-called insurgents. These were the people who'd supposedly launched an attack on Sanctuary.

These were the people she—and Harvey—had been hunting down.

She realised then where she was standing. She was on a wooden platform. And there was something in front of her.

A noose.

She looked around for Kayleigh, then. She couldn't see her. Didn't know where she was. Part of her felt relieved about that, that she wasn't up here and in danger like her.

But the other part of her...

She felt alone.

And she felt afraid.

"I told you it was time for your judgement," Yuri said. "I told you the decision that has to be made is not my decision alone, but the decision of my people. And they have decided."

Aoife felt her stomach sink. They were going to hang her. They were going to execute her, right here. Just because of her association with Harvey.

She thought about pleading. Thought about begging. But she knew that would only be giving them what they wanted.

She knew there was nothing she could say to win these people round. Not after all they'd been through. Not after all they'd suffered.

"Step forward," Yuri said. "Step forward into the noose. Do what has to be done."

Aoife shook her head. Gritted her teeth. "You could have been better than you say Harvey is. But you're no different."

Yuri lowered his head. "The decision of my people, just like I said."

Aoife held her ground. But then she felt the hands on her back, pushing her closer to that noose. "You could have let me try speaking with him. You could have worked through this. We could have found a way to figure something out. The one person who could help you, and this is how you treat us?"

"Neck in the noose," Yuri said. "Now."

Aoife felt tears rolling down her cheeks. But not tears of self-pity or even fear anymore. Tears of anger.

She looked around at the crowd. "Is this what you want?" she shouted. "Our people are no different to yours. We didn't know about this war. We only knew what we were being told. You'll see us all die too? You'll keep on being pawns in this war? Well, shame on you. Shame on fucking you."

She spat off the platform, down onto the ground below.

And she felt the rope stroking her neck. The noose, so close.

The man behind her, pushing her right towards it. Nowhere to go now. Nowhere to run.

"I could speak to him," Aoife said. "I could speak to him and hold him accountable for what he's done. But instead... instead you're going to lead your people to extinction. All of them."

Yuri didn't say a word. Just looked on, as stoic as ever.

"I'm sorry for what Harvey has done. I'm sorry for believing his lies. But how is this better? How?"

"Neck in the noose, Aoife."

She tried to push back. Tried to resist.

But it was already too late.

Her neck was in the noose.

"Hang me then," Aoife shouted. "Fucking hang me. I'm the only one who can help you. I'm the only one who can get to Harvey. I'm the only one who'll let him close enough to kill him. But hang me. You're no different. You're no better. You're savages. I can help you get to him, but you're savages. Just like him."

The crowd stared up at her.
Yuri looked away.
"I could help," Aoife gasped. "I could help. But…"
She didn't finish what she was saying.
She heard a bang.
The floor underneath her gave way.
And she fell into the abyss.

CHAPTER TWENTY-EIGHT

It all happened so fast.

Aoife felt herself falling. Felt the floor beneath her feet giving way. Felt the noose around her neck tightening its grip as she descended through the air.

And in that split second, it was exactly as she'd imagined, the whole life flashing before her eyes thing. Time slowing down. Seeing herself as a child, holding an ice cream. Or getting her GCSE results and feeling so proud.

And there were the bad memories, too. The memories of Mum. Of Dad. Of Seth. The memories of Max. And of Kayleigh. Of making friends and losing friends.

She saw it all, and she felt both happiness and sadness rising within her simultaneously.

And that realisation that life, for all its ups and downs, was the most precious thing.

Experience was the most precious thing of all.

And all of that was going to end.

All of that was going to—

The rope tightened around her neck.

She braced herself for the final moments. For the suffocating pain.

And for the lights to go out, once and for all.

And then she heard a snap.

For a second, just a split second, she thought it was her windpipe. Or maybe even her spine.

But then she slammed against the stony ground and coughed and spluttered everywhere.

She lay there on her knees, hands on the ground. Coughing. Shaking. All her surroundings felt like they'd faded into the background. None of it seemed to matter, not anymore.

All that mattered was that she was still here. She was still alive.

For how long? She had no idea. But she *was* here, and that was something.

That was everything.

She pushed herself up. Saw the crowd of people staring over at her. Some of them had hands over their mouths. Some were chatting amongst themselves, baffled, confused. Others were shouting things. Swearing at her. She wasn't out of the woods yet, that was for sure.

She went to stand when she felt hands on her shoulders and then under her arms, lifting her to her feet.

She stood there. Supported by someone right behind her. She wanted to make a break for it. Wanted to fight. But she was completely out of energy. Completely exhausted. Probably the trauma of what had happened, mostly. The trauma of almost fucking *dying*. Yeah, that could have an impact.

She felt that person holding on to her. And she half-expected them to drag her back up to the top of the platform. 'Cause it was a freak accident. The rope didn't usually snap like that. She wasn't going to get lucky twice.

"Well," Yuri said. So it was him holding on to her. "It looks like someone's looking down on you today."

Aoife opened her mouth. Tried to gasp something. Something stubborn and defiant. But she couldn't say a word.

He turned her around, then. Turned her, so she was looking right into his eyes. And she could tell from the way he was looking at her that there was a different character to his experience now. That he looked at her differently.

"I can... I can help you," Aoife gasped. "I can... Harvey. He's... I can help you."

And she meant it. She wasn't just saying these words because she was in deep shit and wanted to get out. She was saying them because she saw the trauma that Yuri's people had suffered. She'd seen the pain they'd been through, and she had no reason to doubt them. So many people couldn't be lying about one thing.

She didn't know the extent of what Harvey was responsible for. She didn't know to what degree Yuri was exaggerating. And she still couldn't quite accept that Harvey was personally responsible for the explosion at Sanctuary. The one that killed so many of their people.

But she needed to confront him. And that's all she could promise.

"If you let me get to him," she said. "If... if you let me talk to him... I can make him answer to what he's done."

"He'll never answer to what he's done."

"But the people there. The people back home. They... they're good people."

"They're killers."

"They're blind. Just like I was. But if they see. If they understand... then they won't let Harvey get away with it. We... we have a system of justice at Sanctuary. And if Harvey's done what you've said he's done... he isn't immune to that."

Yuri shook his head. But Aoife could see he was in turmoil. She could see he was conflicted. She could see he wanted to punish her because she was one of the ones who'd stood with Sanctuary against his people. But at the same time, she could see that he saw her as useful. She could see his problem was with Harvey and not with his people.

But Aoife knew far too well that it was sometimes difficult to separate the crimes from the group even when just an individual was responsible.

"Let me help you," Aoife said. "Let... let me help your people. I might be... I might be the only one he'll listen to. The only one who can."

Yuri looked into her eyes.

Then he looked up at his people.

He sighed.

"You can help," he said. "But there's only one way you can."

Aoife frowned. Still in disbelief that he'd actually granted her something of respite.

"How?"

"You kill him," Yuri said. "You get to him, and you kill him. By sunset. Or your friend Kayleigh dies."

CHAPTER TWENTY-NINE

Aoife stood at the edge of Yuri's community and had no fucking clue what would happen next.

The sun was rising. It was bright now. Crisp morning. Birds singing. In normal circumstances, it might actually seem quite peaceful. Quite calm.

But Aoife's stomach wouldn't stop turning. Her heart wouldn't stop racing.

Because she knew exactly what was expected of her.

Yuri stood by her side. Looked at her with a calm, firm gaze.

"Sunset," he said. "When it goes dark. That's when you've got 'til."

Her stomach turned some more. For as much as she didn't like the sound of Harvey as had been described... she had serious reservations about killing him. Because she'd trusted in him. She'd believed in him for so, so long.

And now the second the leader of the insurgents claimed he was responsible for all the goddamned ills of the world, she was supposed to just drop her faith in him and kill him without even giving him a chance to speak? A chance to give his version of events?

It just didn't feel right. She didn't believe In not giving people a chance to give their side. A chance to speak.

Especially Harvey.

"I can't express myself any clearer," Yuri said. "If you don't do this, your friend's blood will be on your hands."

"Sounds awfully diplomatic. You're really making an endearing image of yourself."

"I wish there were a better way. And I'm not trying to make myself the hero. The protagonist. I'm thinking about my people. The very survival of my people. Taking Harvey out is the start of that."

"And you really expect the people of Sanctuary to just stop coming for you because Harvey dies?"

"What?"

"Think about it. I go in and take him out. What do you think they'll say? They'll just think you've got to me. They'll pin me up as a defector, something like that. You really think it'll change anything?"

"I don't see what other option we have."

"You let me speak to the people. You let me explain exactly what Harvey's responsible for. You make him answer to his crimes. This violence has to end."

Yuri shook his head. Sighed. "Look. I see your point. I understand where you're coming from completely. You do whatever you have to do to help our people. But Harvey surviving is a non-negotiable. And the time you've got to do it is non-negotiable, too. So, you'd better get moving, and you'd better get thinking how you're going to do this. Time's ticking."

Aoife shook her head as she stared into his eyes. There were so many better ways they could go about this, surely. There were so many other options. There were better ways of going about this.

But then she stepped into Yuri's shoes. And she wondered if she'd play this any differently if she were him. Because if Harvey was how he said he was, then he didn't sound like one for diplomacy. And besides. She knew just how strong the feelings were towards the insurgents from Sanctuary. She knew just how trigger-happy they would be, especially so soon after the attack the other day.

"If you had some kind of evidence," Aoife said. "Some kind of tangible evidence what you're saying's true... that might help me."

Yuri looked back at his people. Then ahead, back at Aoife. "You tell them about the children here. You tell them about the women and the men who've been left without family. You tell them about how we're living. And you tell them the truth about Harvey. About his wife and what happened between us. About his grudge. You tell them whatever you need to tell them. If they want to see the truth, they'll see the truth."

Aoife wished she had more to go on. But she just nodded. It was all she could do.

"And you give him this," Yuri said.

Aoife saw Yuri holding something. A necklace, by the looks of things. "What is it?"

"He'll understand," Yuri said. "It belonged to Caroline. Ross, my son, he took it from her when she died. I want you to give this to him and I want you to look into his eyes when you do."

Aoife felt a shiver run down her spine.

"Now you'd better get going," Yuri said. "You don't have much time."

"Can I ask one thing of you?"

"You're asking a lot by being alive still."

"Kayleigh," Aoife said. "My friend. Can I at least speak to her? Before I leave?"

Yuri shook his head. "You want to see her again; you do what I'm asking of you."

"Please," Aoife said. "It's all I ask. I just want to reassure her. I just want to reassure her of what I'm doing. That I'm going to get her out. Please."

Yuri opened his mouth and looked like he was going to protest. Then he shook his head. Sighed. "A minute. That's all I'm giving you. But don't think I'll be adding it on to your time."

Aoife nodded. "Thank you."

He turned. "Now come on. Better get a move on if you want to get everything done in time."

Aoife followed Yuri through the community. Followed him past the tents, which had fires lit outside. She followed him past the staring eyes of so many people, peering up at her like she was some kind of phantom. Some kind of monster.

She followed him until, eventually, she reached a garage right at the back of the community— a different one to before—overgrown, covered with foliage, and she stopped.

Yuri looked at her. Narrowed his eyes. "One minute. And then out of here."

Aoife nodded.

"And if you try anything stupid, I'll know. I promise I'll know."

"Trust me. It's the last thing I'd do."

"Good," he said.

He opened the door to the dark, damp garage.

Then he held out a hand.

Aoife walked to the door, and she took a deep breath.

Kayleigh sat in the middle of the garage.

Hands tied behind her back.

Ankles tied.

Staring back at her with wide, bloodshot eyes.

"Kayleigh," she said.

CHAPTER THIRTY

"Kayleigh," Aoife said.

Kayleigh stared back at her. She was gagged. Hands tied behind her back. Ankles tied, too. Bound to that chair. And Aoife's mind was in override. She wanted to help Kayleigh. She wanted to be able to do something for her now. Something that would make things easier for her.

But Yuri was staring over at her. And she only had a minute.

There was nothing she could do in that amount of time. Absolutely nothing at all.

So she had to think.

She walked over to Kayleigh. All the time, she scanned the room for some sort of crack in the foundations. Some fault in the brickwork. She looked for some way she could get in here and get Kayleigh out of here before midnight tonight.

Because that's absolutely what she had to do.

She couldn't just throw Harvey out without at least giving him a chance to explain himself.

She couldn't just kill him.

Because, sure. He didn't exactly sound like the nicest of guys, according to Yuri's accusations. According to the picture he'd painted of him.

But she also didn't think Yuri's approach was the most practical or pragmatic.

So she was taking matters into her own hands.

Getting Kayleigh out of this mess.

And then she'd decide what she was going to do about Yuri and Harvey and how she was going to do it.

"Thirty seconds," Yuri said.

Fuck. Half a minute gone already? Shit. Thirty seconds gone, and already she'd not even had the chance to speak to Kayleigh properly.

She walked up to her. Crouched opposite her. Put her hands on her legs, looked into her eyes, and got as close as she could so she could speak without being listened to.

"I don't know how to say this," Aoife said. "But they're making me kill Harvey. They're making me go back and kill him by sunset. And if I don't... they're going to kill you."

Kayleigh just stared at her blankly. No reaction from her at all.

"Twenty seconds," Yuri said.

"I'm going to get you out of here. So be ready. Be ready because I'm not going to let you down. I'm not going to let you die. One way or another... I'm not going to leave you behind."

"Ten seconds," Yuri said.

She saw Kayleigh looking away from her now. Staring into the corner of the garage. Into space. And Aoife just wanted her to look into her eyes. She just wanted Kayleigh to show her some sign that she forgave her. That she didn't despise her.

As much as Aoife knew she deserved it for getting them both embroiled in this mess in the first place.

"I won't let you down," Aoife said. "But I'm sorry. I'm so sorry. I'll make it up to you, and I'll end this mess. I'll sort it. One way or another."

Kayleigh glanced at her, just for a split second.

Then she looked away again. Right into that corner again.

"Time's up," Yuri said. "Out of here, right this second. And get a move on with what you've got to do. You know exactly what that is."

Aoife lowered her head.

Kayleigh still staring off into the right, off into space.

"I won't let you down," Aoife said.

She turned and started to walk back towards Yuri, who stood at the door. Staring at her. The light behind him.

She wished she'd been able to do more for Kayleigh. She wished she'd been able to help her somehow. Or at least given her a shot of getting out of here.

But it looked like she was up shit creek without a paddle.

Didn't mean she wasn't going to try, though.

She walked right up to Yuri and stopped before him.

"You ready?" he asked.

Aoife looked back at Kayleigh.

Saw her staring into space, still. Up to the right of this garage.

Then she turned around to face Yuri when she saw something.

Kayleigh wasn't just staring into space.

There was a vent.

A ventilation shaft on the ceiling, right above her.

A little slither of light shining through.

She saw that ventilation shaft, and she wondered. A plan started to form in her mind.

A glimmer of hope formed in her mind.

She looked at Yuri, took a deep breath, and nodded.

"Ready," she said.

"Good," Yuri said. "Now get to work on Harvey. For your own sake. For your people's sake. For my people's sake. And for your friend's sake."

Aoife was going to ask some serious questions of Harvey, one way or another.

But one thing was for sure.

She wasn't going to let Kayleigh be a bargaining chip.

She looked back at Kayleigh, then up at that vent, and then she followed Yuri back out into the light.

It wasn't going to be easy.

But she knew exactly what she needed to do.

CHAPTER THIRTY-ONE

Aoife made sure nobody was watching her when she turned off the road back to Sanctuary and looped back into the woods towards Yuri's camp.

She knew it was a risky as fuck move. One sniff that she was doing what she was doing, and both she and Kayleigh would be dead.

But one thing was for sure. She wasn't having Kayleigh used as a bargaining chip. She wasn't blindly killing Harvey because of Yuri's threats. Whether his intentions were good or not, whether Harvey was the man he made out to be or not, she still wasn't having him decide all the terms.

She was freeing Kayleigh. She was escaping Yuri's camp with her.

And then the pair of them were going to go back to Sanctuary and confront Harvey together.

Then and only then would she decide what the next step would be.

She didn't do deals with people who threatened to kill her friends.

She kept low and crept through the tall grass. She could hear voices up ahead at Yuri's camp. Heard the wind rustling against the leaves of the trees all around her, and it felt like people were moving. Felt like there were eyes on her. Like someone was watching.

She knew there was a good chance there were people out here watching. She'd seen a few surrounding the camp when she'd left about an hour ago. But she figured it was more likely they'd followed her to track her progress, to make sure she was following the plan to the letter.

Harvey was to be dead by sunfall. And somehow, that news had to be transmitted back to Yuri.

For such a specific plan, there was still a lot of vagueness about the whole situation.

And it made her feel... well. Unsure. Uncertain.

She twiddled at the necklace Yuri had handed her. The one he'd told her to give to Harvey. A necklace belonging to one of his sons, Ross. The one his wife Caroline died wearing. A speck of blood splashed across it from when Ross was killed.

She still couldn't believe it. Couldn't accept it.

Harvey wasn't a monster.

Right?

She peered across the camp, over towards the garage where Kayleigh was being kept. There weren't many people about that she could see. Most of them were in the camp, sitting by fires, cooking, surviving. None of their attention seemed to be on the outside.

Which meant she had a perfect opportunity.

She had to get around the back of the garage. And then she had to climb up onto it and then find a way to drop down the vent and get inside to save Kayleigh.

They could use the chair she was tied on to climb back out. It looked tall enough.

At least she fucking *hoped* it was tall enough. That'd be a right old spanner in the works.

She clenched her jaw and waited there in the long grass until she was absolutely sure she was safe to move.

The second she got up and made her way towards that garage, she saw movement right up ahead.

She stopped. Froze solid. Didn't move a muscle.

Someone walking right past her.

One of Yuri's people.

She watched him pass by, step by step.

Don't turn around. Please don't fucking turn around…

But then it happened.

They started to turn.

And Aoife could do nothing but fall back to the grass and hope the bloke hadn't seen her.

She lay there. Flat on her stomach, heart racing.

The man looked over in her direction. For a second, it looked like he peered right into her eyes.

Then he turned again and kept on walking.

She stayed as still as she could, even though she couldn't stop shaking. Fuck. That was close. Too close.

She waited there a while, then realised she had to get a move on. Not only was time of the essence, but there was nothing stopping that bloke walking right back. Or another of Yuri's people heading this way.

She looked through the trees, towards where that bloke headed.

And then she pushed herself back to her feet and moved as quickly and quietly as possible towards that garage.

She heard voices to her left. Footsteps, so close. She daren't look at them for fear they might look back at her. She was in deep as it was now. She just had to keep going. Had to get there.

And then had to get the hell out of here.

She ran quicker towards the back of the garage.

When she reached it, she slammed against the brick wall at

the back of it. Closed her eyes, took a few deep breaths as sweat trickled down her face.

"You've got this. You can do this."

She took a few more breaths to steady herself when suddenly she realised she had another obstacle on her hands. The garage roof. It was too high for her to scale.

She looked up the side of it and saw protruding bits of old metal pipe. It wasn't a lot, but it would be enough. It *had* to be enough.

She went to climb when she heard a voice heading her way.

"Just go check it out, Stan," a woman said. "I definitely saw something."

Aoife's entire body seized up.

Fuck.

They were onto her.

She climbed up the side of the garage. Tried to hold on to the protruding pipe but with no luck. Just kept on falling back off. Kept on losing her grip on it.

She gripped harder. Tried to get some leverage on the brick.

But all the time, those footsteps got closer.

"Shit," she whispered.

She looked around. Looked for a brick she could hold onto. One that was sticking out or something. Or somewhere close that she could hide for now.

But she knew she didn't have the time.

She knew it was now or never.

Unless...

She looked up at the top of the garage.

Then back over her shoulder, towards the woods.

Maybe she had to give up on Plan A, for now.

Maybe she had to go.

Maybe she had no choice.

But no.

She wasn't leaving Kayleigh behind.

She wasn't letting her be used as a pawn.

It might be your only choice...

She stood there, hands to the garage wall, and heard those footsteps getting closer, as her heart beat faster, faster.

And as she looked at that wall, knowing Kayleigh was so near yet so far, she realised she had no choice.

"I'm sorry, Kay. I'll come back for you."

She went to turn around and run away when she heard a voice right behind her.

"Not another move," he said.

CHAPTER THIRTY-TWO

"Not another move or you're finished."

Aoife heard that voice, and her stomach sank.

She froze. Stared at the trees ahead. Heart racing. Fists clenched.

"Seriously," the man said. "Not another fucking move."

Fucking hell. She'd been stupid. Stupid for coming back here and stupid for getting herself caught. And now she was going to get both her and Kayleigh killed.

And besides. Harvey was never going to be able to answer for the crimes he'd been accused of. Yuri's people were going to die. So many people were going to die. All because of this decision.

She heard the footsteps getting closer.

"What the hell you think you're doing sniffing around here?" the man said. It wasn't Yuri, at least, which was something. She figured he'd just kill her right on the spot. "You're supposed to be a long, long way away from here by now."

Aoife kept still. She wanted to run. But she didn't know if this man was armed. And she didn't want to take her chances of being shot.

"Yuri ain't gonna be happy when he sees you back here. He

showed too much faith in you in the first place, Sanctuary scum. If it was down to me, I'd have killed you and that blonde bitch on the spot. 'Cause you can't be trusted. None of you can be trusted."

Aoife heard those words, and she knew she had another choice. A choice about explaining why she was here. About being honest.

It might backfire. It might not work.

But what other options did she have right now?

She took a deep breath.

This better work.

And then she turned around, hands raised.

"Hey," the man said. He was unusually tall and gaunt. He was holding a pistol. "I told you not to move a muscle."

"I'll level with you," Aoife said. "I'm here to save my friend."

The man's smile turned up, revealing a set of yellow-stained teeth. "Knew it. I knew we couldn't trust you."

"I'm here to save my friend because Yuri told me to get to Harvey the best way I could. I believed that was with Kayleigh. Not with her here as a bargaining chip. As a pawn."

The man narrowed his eyes. His pistol right on her. "That wasn't part of the deal."

"You don't make the rules. Neither does Yuri. The way I see it, we're both caught in a civil war between two individuals. Harvey and Yuri. Why should people have to keep on dying because of the grudge they have against each other?"

"You're full of shit," the man spat. "I've seen people die. Seen them hunted down by you scum."

"And I've seen people die at the hands of your people, too. Good people."

"The explosion wasn't—"

"Not just the explosion. Other times, too. And not always in self-defence, either. When you captured me and Kayleigh in the woods. Good people died then, too. Good people had their throats slit. And don't go telling me for one moment that was some kind of optical illusion because I know what I saw. I know exactly what I saw."

The man gritted his teeth. He didn't exactly look for turning. But he at least looked like he was actually *thinking* about Aoife's words, now. Her perspective.

"I really, really understand why you hate me and my people," Aoife said. "But you have to see things from our side, too. And right now... all I can say is I want my friend out of the crossfire. And if you... if you let me help her, I will speak with Harvey. And I will make sure the people of Sanctuary know about these accusations, too. I'm sure my word doesn't count for much to you. But it's all I've got to give."

The man held the pistol. Stared at her. He was so, so close to her now.

"If your word's all you've got to give, then how the hell am I ever supposed to trust you?"

She opened her mouth to say something else, then realised she would be falling on deaf ears trying to get through to this guy.

So she had to try something else.

"You won't shoot me."

The man narrowed his eyes. "Huh?"

"I said I don't think you'll shoot me."

"And what makes you so fucking confident about that?"

"Because as much as you despise me... you need me. Yuri needs me. I'm the best chance he has at taking Harvey out. And the way things stand, I've technically not done anything wrong. You shoot me right now, and your chance is up."

"Bullshit," the man said. "Get on your fucking knees right this second."

But Aoife didn't.

She stood there, stared into this man's eyes. Fully aware that this was risky as hell. Tantamount to suicide.

But what other choice did she have when she was backed into a corner?

"You let me walk away from here with Kayleigh. Or you fire a bullet at me, and it's over. All of it is over. Your best shot at taking Harvey out, and it's gone. Do you really want that on your conscience?"

"Don't talk to me about conscience," he said.

"Then let me get to my friend. Look away. Just look away for a few minutes. That's all I ask. Lives will be saved. On both sides. And... and I can't do this without her."

He narrowed his eyes. Lifted his pistol, pointed it right at her head with his shaking hands.

Aoife was acting on pure adrenaline now.

"Let me get my friend, and let us leave this place. It's all I ask."

The man shook his head.

Then he looked away.

Tightened his finger on the trigger.

Aoife braced herself for the blast.

Braced herself for her bluffing to fall apart.

"I'm sorry," he said.

And then she heard the deafening bang fill the silent air.

CHAPTER THIRTY-THREE

Aoife heard the blast, and she knew what it meant.

The deafening ringing of gunfire echoing in her skull. Piercing, so loud it felt like it'd burst right through her eardrums. He'd pulled the trigger. He'd pulled the trigger, and he'd done what she hadn't expected him to do, but what's always been a risk: he'd killed her.

But...

She was still thinking.

And other than the ringing in her ears, she didn't feel any pain or discomfort.

She was still alive.

She opened her eyes, which she'd squeezed shut instinctively, and she saw him standing right before her.

He had his pistol raised into the air. And he was looking right into her eyes.

"What..." she started.

"You have about a minute to get your friend out before someone comes to investigate the gunshot," he said. "You'd better get moving."

Aoife couldn't move. She was completely rooted to the spot.

"Your time's ticking," he said.

She didn't even think.

She ran. Ran to the side of the garage this time, running into the same problem as before. Leverage. She couldn't get up. She couldn't climb.

She could hear shouting cutting through the ringing in her ears now. Hear footsteps heading this way.

She had to stay focused. She had to think quickly. She was running out of time.

She searched the garage. Searched for any place she could climb up. But she kept on coming back to those protruding pipes. And she knew that was going to be her only shot.

"Better hurry," the man said. Staring at her, pistol still in hand. "You haven't got much time left."

"Fuck," she said.

She found herself facing the garage back wall again. And this time, she knew there was no backing out. She knew she had to climb the wall. She knew it was now or never.

"Fuck it," she said. "Here goes nothing."

She grabbed one of the sharp pipes sticking out of the brick-work. Put all her weight onto it.

And then she heaved herself up.

It wasn't easy. But she felt like she had more leverage this time. Fuck, probably the panic of the whole situation helping out a bit.

She dragged her foot up the side of the wall, scraping it on the rugged brick in the process, grazing it. She winced through the pain, head still spinning, ears still ringing, time running out.

She got her foot onto the broken pipe.

And then she knew she only had one more move to make.

Reach out for the garage roof.

Get up there.

Then get to Kayleigh.

She went to grab the garage roof when she felt the pipe below her foot snap away.

She felt herself falling. Felt herself descending to the ground below.

But her fingertips were on the edge of the roof.

She clutched on. Wincing. Heart racing. Holding on by a thread.

"Come on, Aoife. Come on."

She pulled herself up with all her force.

Dragged herself harder than she thought she was capable.

And then she shuffled onto the garage roof.

She wanted to lie there for a few seconds. Wanted to stay there and catch her breath.

But she knew she didn't have any time to waste.

She stood up. Ran over to the metal grating on top of the garage. Had a horrible image of it being pinned into place and not being able to get in...

But when she reached it and grabbed it, it fell right away.

She stared down into the darkness of the garage below.

"I'm coming for you, Kay," she said.

She didn't know how the hell they were going to get out of this mess.

But she was going to find a way.

She held her breath and dropped down into the darkness.

She looked around. Looked to her left and her right.

But then, a crippling sense of dread surrounded her.

"Kayleigh?"

She walked around the garage.

Looked for the chair Kayleigh was sitting in.

Looked for Kayleigh.

But the more she looked, the more she searched the darkness, the more a horrifying realisation began to set in.

Kayleigh wasn't here.

She stood there. Heard the footsteps approaching outside.

She didn't understand. She'd been in here. She'd been in here, and she'd managed to fight her way back to her.

And the man outside...

He was helping her.

Wasn't he?

She stood there in the darkness, no hope of getting out of this room at all, when the door opened, and light crept inside.

She squinted. Couldn't see who was there at first. Just a silhouette.

And then she heard Yuri's voice.

"Just as predicted," he said. "Thank you for proving everything we suspected of you."

CHAPTER THIRTY-FOUR

Aoife saw Yuri's silhouette in the garage door, and she knew she was in deep shit.

She'd screwed up. Big time. She'd broken her way into the garage via the hatch on top. She'd risked everything to come back here and get Kayleigh out of this mess. Because she wasn't playing on Yuri's terms. If she was going to confront Harvey, she wanted to do it with Kayleigh by her side. She didn't want to just blindly take him out or assassinate him. She didn't see how that would work in the long run. It'd only lead to more uprising. More death. She knew Harvey. And she knew she needed to handle this sensitively, where the people of Sanctuary were concerned.

But she wasn't going to get a chance. Because Yuri was standing in her way. And there were people around him.

And from the looks on their faces, they weren't going to be too keen to let her out of this garage—or letting her escape—any time soon.

"You need to know why I did this," Aoife said, sensing she had a fight for her life on her hands here and knowing full well that the only way she stood the remotest chance of getting out was by being honest.

Yuri walked into the garage towards her. His large stature blocked any way out. She looked up at the opening on the garage roof, but she knew there was no way she'd reach it.

"Did you really think we'd be so stupid?" Yuri asked, ignoring Aoife's attempts to tell the truth.

"Yuri," she said, backing up. "I did it because I—"

"Leaving her in a garage you knew the exact location of? And a garage with a structural defect, all the same? You walked right into it. You could have helped us. But even with everything you know about Harvey, everything you know about the kind of man he is, you just couldn't help yourself, could you?"

He walked towards her. More of his people joined him now, filling the garage, completely blocking the door.

Aoife carried on backing away. Searching for some kind of escape route. Some way out.

But there was nowhere.

She was trapped in here.

Completely trapped.

"We gave you a chance. A chance more than you deserved. A chance to really help bring about change. And look how you threw it away."

"You didn't give me a chance," Aoife said.

Yuri kept walking towards her.

"You didn't give me a choice. You sent me on a suicide mission. A suicide mission to satisfy some lust for revenge you have. All because of your personal shit with Harvey. You know for a fact Sanctuary will retaliate. You know damned well more people will die this way. But you chose this way anyway because of what Harvey's done to you. You chose for people to die—your own people—because of him."

He launched at her at full speed then, out of nowhere. Grabbed her hair and slammed her against the brick wall, started squeezing her throat. "I did what I did because my people's survival is at stake."

"So you keep saying," Aoife shouted. "But the way I see it... the only thing at stake here is your grudge with Harvey. I'm not discounting your reasons for hating him. I'm not belittling those at all. I know what he did to you was awful, horrible, and wrong. But you're not even giving me a chance to change things. Because... because I don't think you want me to. Because you can't bear the thought for one moment that we might not all be the evil monsters you've made us out to be. Just like you aren't the monsters you've been made out to us. And you can't bear that."

She saw him staring at her. Right into her eyes. Could see the way his eyes were twitching, as he held on to her hair, as his hand around her throat tightened. As his grip on her neck got firmer, and she struggled to breathe.

And she could see the humanity in there, hidden beneath the trauma. Hidden beneath that lust for revenge—a lust that Aoife knew damned well could run so, so strong.

"Think of your kids," Aoife said. "Is this what they'd really want from their dad? Really?"

She knew it was a risky one. Half of her expected him to choke her harder for that. To beat her to a pulp and leave her bleeding out on the floor.

But the other half...

She saw his eyes turning more and more bloodshot as her vision faded, as breathing became impossible.

She saw him shaking his head as tears started to fall from his eyes.

She waited for him to choke her, to strangle her, to finish her off, when he dropped her to the floor.

He walked away. Shouted. Screamed out, right in the middle of the garage, the rest of his people looking at him with confusion. With fear.

Aoife coughed. Spluttered on the floor in front of her. She

kept on looking up as tears rolled from her eyes. Looking up at Yuri as he lay there in a heap, crying on the floor. As people approached him, only for him to shout at them, for him to scream at them to get away.

"I just want him to suffer," he bawled. Showing more emotion than he'd ever shown before. "For what he did to my children. I just... I just want him to suffer."

As much as she disliked the man, Aoife found herself following instinct and doing something she didn't expect herself to do.

She got up and walked over to him.

She stopped at his side and put a hand on his back.

"I know," she said, comforting him. "I'm sorry. I'm so, so sorry."

And then, against all odds, Yuri softened, and he fell into her arms, and he cried.

oife had no idea how long she spent stroking Yuri's back, comforting him as he cried.

But as she crouched there in the darkness of the garage, just the two of them alone in here now, she knew that things were going to be very different from here on out.

Yuri hadn't said a word to her for God knows how long. She hadn't said a word to him, either. Just stroked his back and told him it was okay. That she was sorry. That she understood.

She didn't want to say anything else. She got the impression he'd been bottling his emotions for a long, long time. The loss of his sons, Ross and Ben. The way Harvey had taken them from him so cruelly. The festering revenge, building up inside him ever since that day.

Aoife knew what it felt like to want revenge. She knew exactly what it felt like. She thought of Max, and to this day, her blood still boiled when she thought of Grace and what she'd done to Max. How she'd killed him so ruthlessly.

But at the same time, she'd done awful things to Grace, too. So she understood. She completely understood.

That said. Losing two kids... that was a whole other level of savage.

"Ever since that day," Yuri said, the first thing he'd said in a long time. "All I've wanted is to see Harvey burn for what he took from me. For what he did to those poor boys. And—and even though deep down I knew he had to be lying to you people for you to do the things you've done... you have to see things from our perspective. From *my* perspective."

Aoife nodded. She did. She really did. She got it. And she was probably one of the rare few people who *would* get it.

"They were such good kids," Yuri said. "I mean, it goes without saying. But they were. They were so sweet. They were so... wholesome. Losing them in the way I lost them, took an innocence out of the world. A goodness out of the world. And knowing that Harvey was out there, building this community of his, basking in the light, totally untouchable... it pained me every single day."

Aoife didn't say a word. She just nodded. Nodded and listened.

"I've done bad things, Aoife," Yuri said. "Bad things to turn my people against Harvey's. I hold my hands up. I've provoked the people at your place. I've—I've written the headstones of far too many graves of my own people."

"Revenge can be blinding," Aoife said. "I understand. I really do."

Yuri nodded. Sighed. "I know you do. That's what has made things so... difficult. When it comes to you. And your friend. Less so your friend. She seems more... single-minded. But definitely you."

Aoife half-smiled, forcing it anyway. "Funny you should say that."

"Why?"

"Kayleigh always says I was the one who was blinkered. I was the one who had my head in the sand. Who was too afraid to see the cracks in the paradise at Sanctuary. But now... now I don't think I could see things any other way."

"It's hard, isn't it? When everything you thought you believed in comes crashing down."

Aoife nodded. "Tell me about it."

For a moment, they just looked into one another's eyes. Stared at each other. Aoife saw that humanity to his gaze, now. The man underneath the monster he'd made himself out to be.

"I want to help you," she said. "Truly. I... I believe you. I believe what you've said about Harvey. About what he's taken from you. And I believe deep down that you want the best for your people. But the way you're going about it. The way you're both going about it... there has to be another way. And I can help with that. But you are going to have to trust me, too."

"That's not entirely up to me."

"Yes," Aoife said. "Yes, it is. You're your people's leader. They believe in you. They follow you. And if I know what loyalty is like, they'd die for you. But they don't need to. They don't have to believe in me. There'll be people who don't agree. There'll be people who hate you for any kind of decision that paints any 'Sanctuary scum' in a good light. But you know what you have to do, deep down."

He looked at her. Intently.

"What do you think needs to be done?" Yuri asked.

Aoife took a deep breath. She looked out of the darkness of the garage and into the fading light outside.

"I know it's asking a lot of you. But I need you to trust me. And I need you to be patient. Not to be ignorant or stupid. Be prepared all you like. But I do need you to believe in me."

"Then what is it you intend to do?"

She stood there, heart racing, jaw clenched, and she took a deep breath.

"I'm going to go back home with Kayleigh. And I'm going to speak to Harvey. I'm going to make him answer to what you're accusing him of. And I'm going to force a truce between our people. Once and for all."

CHAPTER THIRTY-SIX

Aoife and Kayleigh walked back towards Sanctuary, fully aware of the magnitude of the task at hand—but still no idea how anything would turn out.

It was late now. Dark. Fuck, the thought of it made her shudder. If they were sticking to the original plan, Harvey would be dead now. Or Kayleigh would be dead. In both circumstances, she'd probably be dead either way.

But she'd managed to bargain with Yuri. She'd managed to convince him to at least let her and Kayleigh *try* getting through to Harvey. Getting through to the people of Sanctuary. Of making Harvey answer for what Yuri accused him of and trying to reach some kind of truce.

It all felt odd; she had to admit. Something still didn't feel right about any of this. She wasn't sure who to believe. She wasn't sure who to trust.

She just kept twiddling with the necklace Yuri handed her, kept on walking, and kept on hoping there was some kind of solution to this within reach.

But she felt doubtful.

She wished they had more to go on. Wished they had an ace in the pack, so to speak. As far as evidence went, she was pretty much acting on hearsay right now.

And what was Harvey going to do? Outright admit to what he'd been accused of? She had no idea.

But all she could do was try.

She looked around at Kayleigh, who walked alongside her. Kayleigh hadn't said much since they'd been released from Yuri's camp. Since Yuri granted them a rare pass to leave and attempt things their way.

But Aoife wasn't totally sure where Kayleigh stood. She knew Kayleigh was always sceptical about Harvey and the idyllic illusion of Sanctuary. She always said nobody got to the top without getting their hands a little dirty.

But at the same time, she didn't exactly seem the biggest fan of Yuri and his people, either.

She needed Kayleigh fully on her side if this was to succeed.

"So what's the plan?" Kayleigh asked. As if she was reading her mind.

Aoife swallowed a lump in her throat. It was a good question. The way she saw it, there were no tricks about it. No catches or anything like that. It was about looking into Harvey's eyes and asking him the question. Posing the accusations to him. Seeing how he reacted and whether he was willing to entertain any kind of truce with the insurgents.

And only then could they start thinking about moving forward.

"We speak to Harvey," Aoife said.

"And you're fully convinced he's gonna just let us wander back in?"

"He's... I know Yuri's accused him of things. Of awful things. But, like, this is about ego. It's about revenge. It's about two men fighting each other. Two men who have hurt each other. They've done awful shit. Unforgivable shit. Harvey, more so, I know. But I... I want to believe that he'll answer to what he's done. That he's not just a power-crazy narcissist like so many others. That he'll see the fault in what he's done. And stand down if that's what it takes. Because he has to answer to what he's been accused of."

Kayleigh shook her head. Smiled a little.

"What?"

"Just still getting used to the new you. Used to be so deep in Harvey's bullshit. Now you've had your world shook, and you've gone completely the other way. Proud of you, sis."

Aoife nodded. "It's not about blindly following Harvey or Yuri or anyone. It's... it's about what's right. And ending this conflict. Securing some kind of truce. If we can get Harvey to accept what he's done and stop the attacks on Yuri's people... Yuri has promised he will follow. As long as Harvey is brought to justice, one way or another. As long as he answers for his crimes."

Kayleigh snorted. "All seems good on paper. But let's see how it goes down in practice."

Aoife knew she was right. It all seemed like a good idea. But the reality of the situation was a whole lot harder to navigate.

There was no knowing how easily Harvey would accept what he'd done.

There was no knowing whether Harvey would just willingly accept any kind of truce—or if the people of Sanctuary would be willing to accept some kind of truce.

There was no knowing whether Harvey had even done the things Yuri accused him of.

And there was no knowing just how much Yuri's word could be trusted going forward, either.

She just didn't know what was real or who to trust.

"We're in the middle of an ego war between two vengeful men," Kayleigh said. "The most dangerous place to be sandwiched."

Aoife laughed at that. Despite whatever shit the pair of them were going through, Kayleigh always had the ability to make her laugh.

"We'll get through this," Aoife said. Smilling at Kayleigh.

"You're not gonna start one of your motivational speeches again, are you?"

"Shut up. I don't do motivational talks."

"You definitely do. Every time we're approaching some big moment... seriously. If the world ever gets back on its feet, you should set up some kind of YouTube channel for people with low self-esteem or something."

Aoife shook her head again. Smiled. It felt like a rare shining moment amidst the darkness. A moment to savour. "You're the one who reads all the self-help crap. Anyway. I'm just looking forward to giving Rex a cuddle again. Poor thing."

"Tell me about it," Kayleigh said. "Although maybe not a cuddle. He stinks."

"He... has a distinctive aroma."

"'Distinctive aroma.' You really are full of it when you've convinced yourself about something, aren't you?"

"That's how love works, I guess."

"Tell me about it," Kayleigh said.

There was a way she looked at Aoife when she said those words. The way she held her stare a little longer than was comfortable.

And then lowered her head.

Cleared her throat.

Blushed.

And Aoife felt it. She felt the weight of what Kayleigh had just said. She felt the implications. Heard them, loud and clear.

She wanted to say something back to her as her heart pounded. As her cheeks burned. She wanted to address that awkward moment because how the fuck could anyone let a moment like that just slip by?

But she didn't get to.

Because Kayleigh turned around and pointed up ahead.

"Shit," she said.

Aoife looked around. "What?"

Kayleigh didn't have to tell her.

In front of Sanctuary, right up ahead, she could see a mass of armed troops heading right towards them.

Rifles raised.

"Looks like we're getting quite the welcome party," Kayleigh said.

CHAPTER THIRTY-SEVEN

Aoife saw the mass of armed guards from Sanctuary walking towards her and Kayleigh, and she started to have second thoughts about coming back here.

There were so many of them. All lined up, all illuminated in the moonlight. Seemed far too many for just the two of them. All marching towards her and Kayleigh.

She wanted to tell herself it was just because they'd been missing for days. And maybe Harvey was worried they weren't alone. Maybe he was worried they were being held captive by Yuri or something like that. Maybe he wanted to search them to make sure they weren't bringing any nasty surprises back with them. Explosives, or anything like that.

It made sense. Aoife understood any sort of hesitation. Any sort of caution.

But at the same time, she just had a bad feeling about everything. A bad feeling that Harvey was one step ahead somehow.

"I hope you made some backup plans for this," Kayleigh said. "Our old pals don't exactly look the friendliest right now."

Aoife wanted to tell Kayleigh to shut up. This situation was stressful and daunting enough as it was without her going on at her, giving a running commentary with her sarcastic comments. But she knew it was just Kayleigh's way. Her way of cutting through her own nerves.

Besides. She was only here in this situation because Aoife had led her into it. If they'd turned away from Yuri's camp, if they'd come back home, they would never have known the truth. And they would probably have gone on to live a happier life in the dark.

It was the old red pill, blue pill thing. They could have been happier not knowing the truth.

But it still wouldn't have been right. It was better to know.

Even if that was the more painful option.

She looked back into the trees. For a moment, she thought about running. Just going back to Yuri's camp and getting away from here. Or even just going it alone with Kayleigh. Away from all this. Because it felt like something big was brewing. It felt like something major was on the horizon. Something momentous.

But she looked back around. Saw those armed guards approaching, moving towards them both, rifles raised, and she knew it was already too late to do anything.

She took a deep breath, looked at Kayleigh, and she tried to smile, even though it was difficult.

"We'll be okay. We've got this."

Kayleigh looked back at her. Smiled. "I hope you're right."

Aoife turned around again then to face the oncoming guards.

She took a deep breath and really did hope this didn't go as badly as her gut kept on telling her it might do.

And then she started walking, Kayleigh by her side.

"Not another move!"

A shout. A shout from one of the guards. The one in the middle, by the looks of things. Aoife recognised him. Stephen, he was called. Middle-aged bloke. One of Harvey's loyal bodyguards. Always seemed pretty friendly.

And that was the bizarre thing about all this. These weren't strangers. These weren't enemies. They were people she knew.

And they were looking at her and barking at her like she was a stranger.

Like she was an enemy.

"We're all clear," Aoife shouted. "We're... we're alone."

"Don't make this difficult, Aoife," Stephen said. A bit of desperation in his voice now. "Just do what we say, and this doesn't have to get nasty."

She stood there, torches lighting her and Kayleigh up, and she knew she'd seen the true state of affairs now. They were the enemy. Or at least, they'd been away long enough that Sanctuary didn't trust them.

So as much as Aoife wanted to protest her innocence, she knew there was nothing else she could do but go along with what they were asking of her.

"Shit," Kayleigh said, shaking her head. "Might have to put that reunion with Rex on hold a little while longer."

Aoife really didn't appreciate that one. Again, it just made things too real. She was trying to stay hopeful here. Trying to stay optimistic. Even though everything pointed towards this being the worst possible situation to be in right now.

"Hands up," Stephen barked. "And don't even think of trying anything."

"Really?" Aoife shouted. "You really think we'd do anything?"

"You've been missing for three days. We have reason to believe you were with the insurgents. And then out you walk, out of nowhere. Trust me. Just try not to take this whole thing too personally, and we'll all get by just fine."

Aoife shook her head, but she knew she had no choice. She lifted her hands slowly. Saw Kayleigh do the same.

"Good," Stephen said. "Now, on your knees. And stay on your knees until we come over there. One move, and we'll be forced to act appropriately."

Act appropriately. That's what they called it? That's what they called killing her and Kayleigh?

But again, there was nothing else she could do. She wanted to speak with Harvey. She wanted to look him in the eye and bring up Yuri and everything he'd accused him of.

A part of her thought of telling these guards everything right now. But she knew how it would look. Like they'd been intercepted. Compromised. Brainwashed in some way.

So she got down onto her knees. Onto the damp ground. Crouched right there, right beside Kayleigh. She held onto the grass before her tightly. Listened to those footsteps getting closer, squelching against the damp earth. She wanted to believe she was out of the crosshairs. She wanted to believe that things wouldn't get worse from here. That they couldn't possibly get worse from here.

But she didn't know.

She just didn't know.

She had no idea how long she knelt there when one of the guards searched her. Dragged her to her feet. Scanned her from head to toe.

Trent. One of the guards she got on with. Used to guard the south wall. Went on a few hunts with him.

Barely looking her in the eye now.

"She's clean," he said.

"Kayleigh too."

"Of course, we're clean," Kayleigh said. "We've spent three fucking days in captivity, and this is how you greet us?"

"It's just protocol," Stephen said. "From the top."

The way he looked at Aoife when he said that she knew she would have trouble with Harvey. More than she first imagined.

He was already onto her. He already knew what this was about.

Out of nowhere, Stephen dragged Aoife to her feet, and another of the guards lifted Kayleigh, too.

Then the pair of them stood behind Aoife and Kayleigh, pointed rifles at their backs, nodded at them to walk.

"What the hell?" Kayleigh shouted.

"Just protocol. For our safety and yours. Now come on. The boss wants to see you."

Aoife stood there and looked at the guards surrounding her. All of them with their rifles raised.

She looked at Kayleigh. Then back at the woods behind, back towards Yuri's community.

She didn't know the truth. But she knew what this looked like right now.

The actions of a paranoid man.

She gritted her teeth.

And then she took a deep breath, turned back towards the tall metal walls of Sanctuary, and walked.

It was time to face Harvey, once and for all.

CHAPTER THIRTY-EIGHT

Yuri watched Aoife and Kayleigh being dragged inside Sanctuary, and he held on to the rifle tightly.

It was still mesmerising, seeing all those torchlights. Those artificial lights. Those little beacons of hope. Signs that the power could return. Signs that life could return. He wished he'd been given an opportunity to enjoy the fruits of the labour of so many. He thought back to that day eighteen months ago when he'd arrived on the doorstep of the place with his two boys and how much optimism he'd had. How much hope he'd had.

And how quickly things went sour.

Or at least...

Well.

That was the story he told himself.

That was the story he told himself so, so convincingly.

He held on to his rifle. Stared down the scope. Kept it pointed up ahead at all times. More of his people were beside him. Hiding in the trees. Camouflaged. But closer to Sanctuary than they'd ever been.

More people than he ever thought he'd amass. And more people than Sanctuary ever thought he'd amass, too.

Holding on to their rifles before this so-called "truce" that Aoife had so desperately bargained for.

He snorted a bit at the thought of a truce. Because there was no way he was letting Harvey go. There was no way he was letting him get away with his crimes. There was no way he was going unpunished for robbing him of his life. Truce or no truce, Harvey was a dead man. And Aoife was an idiot if she thought there was anything she could do or say to change that.

But it didn't matter. Because this was war.

It didn't matter that Aoife and Kayleigh were almost certainly going to die at the hands of Harvey the second they let on to the knowledge of the monster he was. Because this wasn't about them. They were just pawns in this game. Useful pawns.

They were just a way of getting to Harvey.

A way of hurting him and showing him how easy it was to muddy his poisonous waters with the truth and how easy it was to turn people against him.

He knew Harvey would care about Aoife. And he knew exactly why. She reminded *him* of Caroline, so she'd sure as hell remind Harvey of her too.

Seeing her confront him, seeing her look him in the eyes when he cared about her, seeing her *judge* him...

It would be salt in Harvey's already paranoid wounds.

And it didn't matter if he killed Aoife and Kayleigh or just locked them away.

It would be merely a reminder that Yuri was on his doorstep and that he would come knocking.

Very, very soon.

He lay there on his stomach and watched as Aoife and Kayleigh disappeared behind the Sanctuary gates.

He thought about the fireworks that were about to explode, and he smiled.

Everything had built to this moment.

Everything had led to this.

"It's almost time," he said.

He thought about the necklace he'd handed Aoife, and he really, really hoped she handed it to Harvey, just as he'd ordered.

They had no idea who—or what—they were messing with.

But they were about to find out.

CHAPTER THIRTY-NINE

Aoife stepped inside the gates of Sanctuary and felt like the proverbial lamb being taken to slaughter.

It was night, but the streets were filled with people. Residents of Sanctuary, all of them staring at her and Kayleigh with torches and candles by their sides. All of them chattering amongst themselves. All of them watching and waiting for whatever events were about to unfold.

And as the guards walked her and Kayleigh through the streets, Aoife saw more faces of people she knew. Faces of people she was friends with. Of people she'd worked with. Looking at her with fear. Like she was some kind of traitor.

What had Harvey told them?

"Come on," Stephen said, gently nudging her in the back. "Keep walking. Don't want to make a spectacle out of this."

She resisted the urge to tell him she was moving quickly enough and walked. She looked at the cracked road before her, the weeds shooting up between the cracks. She didn't want to look the people of Sanctuary in the eyes anymore. Because she felt judged. For what? She didn't know. Only that she felt judged for the knowledge she had.

The knowledge about Harvey.

The truth about Harvey?

Even that was unclear. For an entire community to be hood-winked by him, that seemed impossible.

And yet here she was. And what reason did Yuri have to lie?

He was sincere. He'd broken down. He was a man in the throes of vengeance, sure. But there were few things in life more honest than vengeance.

She felt Stephen turning her and Kayleigh around the corner by the old mini-roundabout near the town square when she saw Harvey.

He was standing there, arms behind his back. At first, Aoife swore she saw him smile.

But then the smile soon dropped, and he walked up to her and Kayleigh. Wordless. Speechless.

But with a look in his eyes like he already knew what they knew.

"Aoife," he said, cutting through the silence. A smile rose on his face. "Kayleigh. It's good to see you both again."

"Quite the welcome party," Aoife said.

"We can't be too careful. Not when you've been deep in insurgent territory for as long as you have been. You know how it is these days."

"Some would say you're worried about something," Aoife said.

Harvey narrowed his eyes. "What's that supposed to mean?"

"I think we need to talk. I think you know... I think you know exactly what I mean."

He stared at her for a few seconds longer than was comfortable. And then he smiled, nodded. "I'm sincere when I say I'm happy to see you back—"

"Then why don't you start being sincere about everything else?" Kayleigh spat.

Aoife glared at her. She wanted her to keep her cool. But she got it. It was hard to contain the anger she felt. Hard for anyone to contain that degree of anger.

Harvey looked over at her. Any form of warmth had fallen from his face. "And what's that supposed to mean?"

"It means exactly what it sounds like," Kayleigh said. "Or do you need reminding?"

"Kayleigh," Aoife said.

"Ross," Kayleigh said. "Ben. Those names not mean anything to you?"

Harvey's eyes widened. For a moment, his face went a completely new shade of pale. He looked like he was going to vomit, right on the spot.

"Yeah," Kayleigh said. "I thought that might be the case."

"How do you... how do you know their names?"

Harvey looked at Aoife now. And as much as she felt in the spotlight, as much as she felt the eyes of this entire community—a community she once called home—burning into her, it was very much just her, Kayleigh, and Harvey right now.

"How do you know the names of my children?"

Aoife opened her mouth to speak. Because... no. that wasn't right. That wasn't what she'd been told. "Your children? Or Yuri's children?"

"Yuri?" Harvey said. "I don't... What are you talking about?"

Aoife heard the whispers picking up. There was an eerie sense of quiet about the place. The sort of quiet that felt falsely safe.

Like something wasn't about to happen. Like things were comfortable in here.

But like something could crawl out of the shadows and strike at any moment.

"What are you talking about, Aoife?" Harvey asked.

Aoife's mouth was dry. She swallowed a lump in her throat. Looked at Kayleigh, who frowned, clearly similarly confused. "We met the insurgent leader. A man called Yuri. He... he claimed you killed his children. A revenge act for an affair with his wife, Caroline. And that you've... that we've been hunting him down ever since. Hunting his people down ever since."

Harvey stared at her. He seemed to be getting paler and paler by the moment.

"He wanted... he wanted me to kill you. But obviously... He wants a truce. He said his people's survival depends on it. There's —there's children. And they're weak. They're weak, and they're hungry and..."

"My children died in a car accident fifteen years ago," Harvey said. "Ben and Ross. The man driving the car who killed them was called Yuri. He was drink driving. He begged me not to report him. Begged me to let him go. But I couldn't. Of course, I couldn't. He went to prison. He lost everything. He spent his life afterwards terrorising my wife and me. *My* wife, Caroline, who died while I was... while I was on deployment years ago. And you're saying he's... he's the leader? Of these people?"

Aoife shook her head. Her mouth was completely dry. She didn't know what to say or think. She didn't understand.

Only that something was wrong.

Something was desperately wrong.

"What did he... what did he say to you?" Harvey asked. Everyone so confused. The crowd looking on, talking amongst themselves. Whispering. Some of them leaving, clearly being spooked by the weird shift in atmosphere.

But most of them staying. Watching. Closely.

"Aoife," Harvey said, stepping forward. "What... what did this Yuri send you here for?"

She reached into her pocket. Pulled out the necklace Yuri handed her. The one with the blood on.

And she put it into his hand.

"He said... he told me to give you this. That you'd understand."

Harvey looked down at the necklace.

Then he looked back up at Aoife, fear on his face. "What—"

She didn't hear him finish.

Because right in front of her, an explosion ripped through the air, tossed her back, and sent her hurtling into the darkness.

CHAPTER FORTY

Aoife felt the back of her head slam against the concrete, tasted blood in her mouth and wondered what the fuck had just happened.

Her ears were ringing. Ringing worse than ever before. A blinding, screeching sound splitting through her skull. Her eyes ached. Her palms were sore, she realised from digging her nails into them. What had happened? What the fuck had just happened?

She opened her eyes, but all she could see was a blurry haze. The metallic taste of blood was getting stronger in her mouth, clinging to the back of her throat. Her heart raced. Her chest felt tight. She could smell smoke and taste something else rusty and damp on her lips.

She didn't know what it was, but she could harbour a guess.

She could harbour a very good guess.

Because she'd been plunged into a situation like this all too recently, and she knew the sound of panic. Of pain. Of confusion.

An explosion.

She sat up. Her back ached like mad. A splitting pain shot down the base of her skull, right towards her stomach. But more than anything, that sense of confusion. That sense of not wanting to look. Of not wanting to see. Of not wanting to know what had happened because the thought of it was almost too much to entertain.

The confusion on Harvey's face when she'd said the names of Yuri's children.

The children Harvey supposedly killed.

Supposedly.

And then handing him the necklace Yuri had given to her, Harvey pushing her back and telling her to get away, and...

She looked up and saw the scene before her, and she felt her stomach sink.

There was a pile of bodies right before her. Or rather, body parts.

Dismembered legs. Arms. Hands.

And heads.

Fragments of skull and bone and flesh, all over the place.

Burning.

Charred.

And in the middle of this scene of exploded bodies, there was a large bloody pool where the explosion had splashed out and ripped through.

The source of the explosion.

A source she couldn't understand.

But a source she couldn't deny.

What was left of Harvey lay in several pieces, two of which were right before her.

Half of his head. Split completely in two by the blast.

And then his hand.

His hand, holding on to that necklace.

The explosion looked like it'd come from that necklace.

The necklace Yuri urged Aoife to hand Harvey.

But how?

How was that even possible?

Aoife stood up. Walked over to Harvey's body. Waded through the smoke. Her head still spinning. The screeching in her ears getting louder and louder. The taste of blood growing more metallic, more intense.

And that crippling sense of dread getting all the more intense every single moment.

What had happened here?

What had happened?

She walked past discarded limbs. Walked past screaming children, some of them wandering along with their clothes burned, with arms dangling off. She walked past people running away in fear, right over to him.

And she stopped, right above him.

Stopped and looked down at that necklace.

Right underneath it, she saw a hole in the ground.

A hole that was filled with fragments of metal.

A hole that looked like it had housed some sort of bomb.

She stood there, sweating, barely able to breathe. The sound started to return now. She wished it hadn't, in a way. Because she could hear more screaming. She could hear crying. And she could hear the pain that she couldn't help feeling *she* had caused.

She looked down at that pendant. And then a sudden bolt of urgency struck her.

"Kayleigh," she said.

She looked around. At the bodies first. Not wanting to see her. Not wanting to know.

But at the same time, knowing she had to.

Because Kayleigh had been standing right beside her.

She'd been standing right beside her, and now she was gone.

She looked around. Searched the bodies. Searched the dismembered hands. Saw the sparkling wedding rings glistening in the flames. Saw the dark blood all over the place. She saw the burst eyeballs and the vacant heads of people she used to know.

And she couldn't help thinking she was responsible for this.

She'd come back here, and she was responsible.

But she couldn't see Kayleigh.

"Kayleigh!" she shouted.

She stepped forward. Went to keep on searching for her. She had to be near somewhere. She had to know she was okay.

"Kayleigh!" she shouted, limping along. "Kayleigh, please."

She staggered forward, head spinning, sounds screeching now. She could hear something else. More blasts. More explosions. Gunfire. Over at the south wall.

And she knew something was happening. Something big.

She knew she'd been fooled again along the way.

And she felt a fucking idiot for it.

She hated herself for it.

She had to get to Rex, and she had to make sure he was okay.

And she had to find Kayleigh and...

She went to walk when she saw Stephen standing there right before her.

He was covered in blood. He looked like he'd been crying. He was holding a gun. Pointing it at her.

"Out of respect for what you were," he said. "You need to leave. Because nobody else will show you the same mercy."

Aoife didn't understand. She didn't get what he was saying. Mercy? For what?

And then it clicked.

How this looked.

It looked like she was responsible.

Like this was an attack.

"But I..."

He lifted the rifle higher and marched closer to her. "Go," he said. "Go now. And never come back. Never."

She thought of Kayleigh.

She thought of Rex.

She thought of this beautiful place she called home.

And as she stood there in the burning ruins of a place she called home, she felt her shoulders slump, and she nodded.

She didn't have a choice anymore.

She wiped her eyes.

Turned around.

And without looking back, feeling nothing but guilt and crippling shame, she walked away from Sanctuary.

CHAPTER FORTY-ONE

Yuri stepped up to the open gates of Sanctuary and smiled.

He took a deep breath of the smoky air. He could almost taste the blood on it if he concentrated closely enough. And that made him even happier.

Because it meant this plan had worked. A plan that had required much debate. A plan that had taken ages to bring to fruition. A plan that had required the utmost patience.

But a plan that he would enjoy the fruits of very, very much.

He looked around at the screaming Sanctuary scum. He looked at the bodies, dismembered, limbs torn off, bones shattered.

And he looked at that bloodied patch, right in the middle of it all, and his smile widened even more.

That cunt.

That cunt Harvey.

The cunt who stole his life from him.

And for what?

Because he'd made a mistake behind the wheel that night. Because, sure, he'd had a few too many to drink.

He'd begged him not to report him. Begged him to let it pass as an accident. Begged him for his life because he had a family of his own. A wife. A son. He'd begged him.

But Harvey showed no mercy.

And Yuri got put inside and lost everything.

He thought back to the day the power went out. The day he knew he could get away with things he wouldn't be able to get away with in a normal world. The day he'd stepped out of those confines where he'd only had one thing on his mind.

Finding Harvey.

Finding him and making sure he punished him truly for what he'd done.

And it had taken longer than planned. Finding him was hard enough. But building a group that was strong enough in number and capable enough of challenging him... yes, that was tough too.

But he'd got there, in the end.

With a little help from his friends, he'd got there.

And he'd stumbled on some rather unexpected prizes along the way.

He thought about Aoife and Kayleigh. He felt no sympathy where they were concerned. As much as they were both more empathetic towards Yuri and his people's supposed "plight," they were dumb. Because they'd fallen for his plan.

They'd gone in there and attacked Sanctuary at its heart.

They'd torn open the doors without realising.

Aoife had gulped all Yuri's sympathetic bullshit just enough for her to believe he *might* be telling the truth.

The shit about the dead brat kids.

The shit about Caroline dying on the road.

Even when he'd tried to hang her.

All of it was for one reason.

To create a believable enough representation of a complex figure of a man.

And Aoife had swallowed it like cum.

And now that place was Yuri's and his people's, once and for all.

He walked through the gates. Looked around at the people running through the streets, desperately trying to get away.

And he smiled.

He thought about the people he'd brought here. The people he'd amassed. Loyal followers. Followers he'd promised a home to and was now delivering on.

"Your time is up," he said. "It's someone else's turn, now."

And then he nodded at his people.

They open fired on the place. Open fired on those still standing. They ran at the Sanctuary guards with knives raised. Some of them fell. Some of them were gunned down.

But for the most part, Sanctuary was not ready for this.

They were reeling from another explosion.

And see, Yuri had more people than he'd been letting on. And he was more armed than he'd been letting on.

He was a more significant figure than he'd been letting on to anyone.

And he'd also had people in here helping out. People who weren't satisfied being at the bottom of the pile of Harvey's hierarchy.

People who wanted more.

His reach went far beyond Sanctuary.

And this was about far, far more than just a grudge. Nice as achieving that vengeance was.

This was about electricity.

About taking this community for himself.

About becoming the most powerful man in the country.

He watched his people shoot and stab and gut everyone without discrimination. Without compromise. And he felt a twinge of sadness. Sadness at seeing the poor innocent kids on the ground, the life drifting from their eyes.

But he took a deep breath and composed himself.

They had plenty more kids who would make this place their home.

He walked to the middle of the bloodied ground, right to the scene of the explosion, right past a leg that looked like it had been ripped away at the knee, and he looked down at the bloody mess that remained of Harvey. Half his skull right there, one eye staring out, shock still clear to see.

His only regret was that he hadn't been able to kill him personally.

But he knew for a fact Aoife had delivered the message he wanted her to deliver.

He reached down. Grabbed the remains of the necklace from his hand.

He took a deep breath, and he smiled.

The greatest part of his plan.

Planting the bomb right in the middle of that square.

Watching Aoife hand him the very necklace he'd ripped from Caroline's neck before he strangled her with it.

A murder that Yuri was never caught for.

A murder that didn't even look like a murder because he'd been very, very careful to cover his tracks.

And the dying realisation Harvey must have experienced that Yuri was responsible for it.

He smirked, and he shook his head.

He was home now.

He lifted his foot and buried it into the remains of Harvey's skull, cracking it on impact.

Home sweet home.

CHAPTER FORTY-TWO

When Aoife left Sanctuary, she didn't stop walking.

It was dark. The night felt like it was dragging on forever. She had no idea how long she'd been walking, only that it felt like days. Weeks. Months.

She just didn't want to think about what had happened at Sanctuary.

Didn't want to think about what had happened to Harvey.

Or to Kayleigh.

Or to Rex.

Or to anyone.

She just walked, the rain lashing down from above, the wind battering her, and tried to focus on one footstep after another.

Tried not to ruminate. Tried not to get lost in thought.

Tried to keep the demons at bay.

The explosion.

The blood.

The gunshots.

Yuri's people swarming in...

And how she'd been double-crossed.

How she'd allowed herself to believe Yuri might be telling the truth all that time.

How she'd bought into his sympathetic tales.

How she'd actually doubted Harvey. A good man. A man who had the best interests of the community at heart. A man who'd lost his children in a car accident, Yuri being the one responsible.

She'd bought into a lie, and now here she was. Alone. Outcast.

Sanctuary blaming her for what had happened.

And rightly so.

She shook her head and traipsed forward. She was on a main road in the middle of... well, she had no idea where she was anymore. The usual sights around her. Abandoned cars, rusty now, many of them stripped of their parts. Cracked pavements. Overgrown gardens and fancy-looking houses with smashed windows. Cafes all boarded up, and petrol stations all burned out from the day of the collapse.

And as Aoife walked, she felt detached from it all, somehow. Like it didn't matter anymore. Like none of it mattered anymore.

Because what was the point of anything anymore?

She'd lost everything. And it was all on her. Every single bit of it was all on her.

Max. Rex. Kayleigh. Harvey.

The very community she called home. The one place she'd felt safe. And the first place she'd felt safe for a long, long time. Even longer than pre-dated the blackout.

All of it, gone.

She kept on walking. She had pain in the bottom of her feet from nasty blisters, which made her limp. She felt sick, her throat filled with the taste of clotted blood. She was exhausted. Freezing cold and wet through.

But she told herself to just keep on walking. Just lifted one foot and planted it after the other.

And again.

And again.

No idea where she was going.

No direction in sight.

She was just walking until she couldn't walk anymore. Walking until she collapsed or reached water, and then she was just going to keep on going and going and going...

She didn't care anymore. She had nothing else to live for. She had no fight left in her body.

Everything was over.

Everything was gone.

And anyone who would make any kind of attachment or connection with her would be better off without her.

She walked down this main street, the rain growing heavier and more intense. She kept on going until the storm stopped, and then she collapsed by some overturned bins, which reeked of rot. She tried to stand up, but her feet were too sore now. She pulled off her shoes and looked at them. Nasty bloody blisters all over her feet.

She tried to stand again and keep going, but it was no use. Tried popping the blisters, but the pain was just so sharp, and even when the fluid came seeping out, she still couldn't walk on them. If anything, it made the pain worse.

She sat there by the side of the road as the rain and the wind picked up again, as she shivered and cried and crouched there in the darkness feeling totally pathetic.

And she knew this was it. She knew that hypothermia would come for her. Or a group of bandits would come for her. Or infection or starvation or dehydration or dogs or whatever would come for her. She knew it. She just knew it.

So she wasn't fighting it anymore.

She knew what the outcome was already, and she wasn't going to fight.

She lay back. Lay back on the tall, muddy grass and stared up at the stars. She told herself she was camping. Camping in the garden like she did when she was little. Hiding in the tent while

Dad stalked around the outside of it, his shadow illuminating the inside of the tent like he was a monster, Aoife unable to stop herself laughing.

Only in the memory, as she lay there crying, it wasn't Dad she saw this time. It was Max.

The only man she'd ever felt this safe with.

"I wish you were here," she said. "I wish... I wish you were still here."

She heard his laughter. Felt the warmth of his hand against her face. Felt his touch and softened inside, completely.

"I'll always be here," he said. "Always."

A tear rolled down her cheek, washed away by the torrential rain.

A smile crept up her face.

And in the bitter cold, a warmth filled her body.

She wasn't alone anymore.

She wasn't suffering anymore.

She saw Max standing there in the light, and she took a step towards him and grabbed his hand.

She wasn't alone anymore.

CHAPTER FORTY-THREE

When Aoife opened her eyes, it was completely bright up above.

The sun beamed down, scorching hot. Her lips felt chapped, and her head ached like mad. She felt sore all over. Aching back. Aching legs. And her feet... oh God, her feet.

For a moment, as she lay there, totally confused, she had no idea where she was. She had no idea what had happened to lead her here. And she had no idea why she was in so much pain.

And something deep inside told her she didn't want to know. That she was better off just closing her eyes again and acting as if nothing had happened. Resisting reality. Resisting a dark truth that felt like it was catching up with her, that was threatening to rear its head once more.

She closed her eyes and basked in the glow of the sun, drifting off into a calm, peaceful state again, when suddenly everything hit her.

Sanctuary.

Yuri.

Harvey.

The attack.

Kayleigh...

She opened her eyes. Glared up at that blinding sun again, which was so bright it made her eyes sting like mad. The memories. She tried to hold them back. Tried to resist them. She didn't want to think about them. Didn't want to let them back in.

But then she couldn't resist them anymore.

The memories of the attack.

The attack that had caused so much death and so much destruction.

The attack that had seen her booted from her home and out on the streets, walking aimlessly.

The attack that had ended life as she knew it.

She lay there and felt the crippling anxiety tighten its grip around her throat and chest when suddenly she became aware of footsteps somewhere close by.

She turned around. Looked over her aching shoulder. She was in a garden in the middle of an estate. A decent-looking semi-detached house right opposite her.

She squinted over towards it, her vision hazy and blurry. She swore she'd heard someone from that direction. Someone close.

Unless she was just imagining things. She was hardly the best judge of reality right now. Everything felt pretty fucking bizarre, that was for sure.

She looked over at that house. Waited for more movement. Waited for another sound.

But there was nothing.

She went to roll back over when suddenly she saw a woman standing right over her, dog by her side.

Aoife scrambled back, jumping out of her fucking skin. "Fuck."

"Awake now?"

For a second, Aoife felt fear. Total fear. Because whoever was here couldn't have good intentions. They'd be a bandit. Or one of Yuri's people, out to hunt her.

But when she saw who was standing right there and who she had by her side, she felt a weight rise off her shoulders.

"Kayleigh," she said. "Rex."

She hugged Kayleigh. Hugged Rex, too. It hurt to hug them both. And Rex sure seemed like he was enjoying it more than Kayleigh was, that was for sure.

"Okay," Kayleigh said, pushing her away. "Okay. Enough of the affection. You stink. You've looked better."

Aoife noticed the cuts across Kayleigh's face. The bruises. And the torn clothes. "Could say the same about you."

Kayleigh nodded. "Yeah, well. Surviving an explosion does that to a person."

Aoife lowered her head. "I'm so—"

"Don't you dare apologise for a thing. Yuri played us for mugs. But even if we hadn't... we weren't to know."

Aoife felt tears welling up. She couldn't look Kayleigh in the eye. "I thought you were dead."

Kayleigh lifted Aoife's chin, smiled at her. "Well, I'm not. I'm here. I'm right here. Question is, what the fuck are you doing lying here feeling sorry for yourself?"

Aoife lowered her head again. She felt ashamed. Ashamed of what had happened. Responsible. "I... They made me leave. They think—they think I'm a terrorist. One of the insurgents."

Kayleigh smirked. "Yuri's people ain't so keen on us either. I barely got away with my life. Bastard."

"How did you find me?"

"Wasn't hard. Tracked you from miles back. Took a few wrong turns along the way, but hey. Looks like I'm an expert tracker these days. Who'd have thought it, hmm?"

Aoife smiled. "I'm proud of you."

She started crying again. She couldn't contain it.

"Hey," Kayleigh said, sounding firmer now. "I get it. Really, I do."

"We had everything. And we lost it all. All because we got

ourselves involved in... in something we shouldn't have. I should never have got us caught like I did."

"Maybe not," Kayleigh said. "But the game's not up. Far from it."

Aoife narrowed her eyes. "What?"

Kayleigh put a hand on her shoulder, which made Aoife wince. "One thing they don't know about us is the shit we've been through. And how we don't give up. No matter what. But another thing they're forgetting is we know exactly where to hit them where it hurts the most."

"I don't understand," Aoife said.

Kayleigh smiled. "The power source."

Aoife could hardly believe what she was hearing. "What? But that's... that's everything we built towards."

"No," Kayleigh said. "Power's nice. Don't get me wrong. I'll miss my luxury showers. But somewhere along the way, we got so caught up in power again that we forgot the best thing we've built wasn't power at all. It's a community."

Aoife heard what Kayleigh was saying. And as cheesy as it was, she heard her.

"But we don't have a community," she said. "Not now they think we're traitors."

"That's where you're wrong," Kayleigh said.

What? Aoife didn't understand. She didn't see what Kayleigh was getting at.

Not until suddenly, out of nowhere, she saw figures emerging.

Emerging from the shadows.

Closing in on the house.

Ten.

No. Twenty. At least.

All of them people she recognised.

Some of them looking weak. Some of them looking like they'd been through hell.

But all of them, Sanctuary.

"We don't need power," Kayleigh said. "Not when we've got each other. Now. Are you ready to get yourself kitted up?"

Aoife shook her head. "Are you really suggesting what I think you're suggesting?"

"Why the fuck not?" Kayleigh said. "The way it stands, the best chance we have of really hurting Yuri is a blow right to his chest. And the biggest blow we can make? Destroying that power source. Now, you know where it is, don't you?"

Aoife thought back to her trips down there with Harvey. "Just... just outside the inner walls."

"Then what the hell are we waiting for?" Kayleigh asked.

Aoife looked around at the people here, those who had joined her side, and she shook her head. "Do we really want to do this?"

"I don't see us standing a chance taking Yuri on. Not with the kind of numbers he's got. Way, way more than I thought. But hell. If we can take the power out, at least it's something, right? What have we got to lose?"

Aoife wanted to shake her head.

She wanted to resist.

But in the end... she could see a kind of logic in what Kayleigh was saying.

A daring kind of logic, but logic all the same.

Kayleigh held out a hand.

All around, Aoife saw the smiling residents of Sanctuary.

Ready to stand by their side.

Not hating her like she'd expected. Not despising her.

But ready to fight.

She took a deep breath.

Then, she grabbed Kayleigh's hand and stepped up.

"I'm ready," she said.

"Good," Kayleigh said. "Then let's go fuck some shit up. We're destroying that damned power source. And we're destroying Yuri. Once and for all."

CHAPTER FORTY-FOUR

Yuri looked out at the streets of Sanctuary and couldn't shake the feeling of concern hanging over him.

It was morning now. A bright, beautiful morning. The air was warm. He could hear birdsong above.

And the most beautiful thing of all?

The sight of his people, standing in the streets.

Standing in their new home.

He stood there in the middle of the main road that ran through Sanctuary, and he smiled. Smiled at the sight of children playing. At fires being extinguished. But more than anything, at the happiness that accompanied discovering power.

Because that's what this was all about, really.

Sanctuary was okay when it came to being a safe place to reside. But it wasn't impenetrable. Yuri and his people had more than proven that fact.

But where Sanctuary's value really lay was in its electricity.

Its power.

He knew the value of power. It was impossible to put a figure on it.

But now they were here, and now they had their hands on a

community charged by electricity, they could begin to attract outsiders to join their cause.

And he'd heard the rumours, too. The rumours of other places like this. Other "districts", as they were known.

Maybe Sanctuary was just the beginning of his empire.

Humanity needed order. And who better a man to instil it?

So far, so good.

But he had a bad feeling.

He looked at the blood on the streets as he walked on through. A bitter taste filled his mouth as he looked down at that blood. The blood of the people he'd killed. The blood of the people he'd ordered to kill. The remains of the bodies that had been blown apart in the explosion, ripped open in the attack.

And yet... something still wasn't right.

"How many did you say there were?"

Trent, one of Yuri's closest, shrugged. "Hard to know. But we're guessin' about fifty bodies. Hard to tell with the state of some of 'em, y'know."

Yuri's stomach tensed at that. Because there were way, way more than fifty people here. Twice that, at least.

Which meant there was twice this community's population unaccounted for.

"And the women?"

Trent looked at the ground, shook his head. "Not a sign."

Yuri gritted his teeth harder at that. He knew the chances the women—Aoife and Kayleigh—had got away was slim at best. But there was still that niggling fear. That nagging suspicion that if they'd got away, if they'd escaped this place, then they might actually still pose some kind of threat... that feeling wouldn't go away.

Because he knew what kind of character Aoife was. He'd seen how much of a fighter she was. She wasn't the kind who was going to give up willingly.

And she'd no doubt have a lot of questions for Yuri.

"I wouldn't worry about it, boss," Trent said. "Like, what can they do, really? This place is ours. If any of 'em comes within a mile of it, we'll blast 'em off the face of the earth."

Yuri nodded. He knew Trent was right. After all, what could the pair of them do to a community as big as Sanctuary?

Especially when he'd gone a long way to convincing the surviving people of Sanctuary that they were both just terrorists?

And yet, at the same time, Yuri couldn't shift that sense of concern.

It ate away at him. The one thing stopping him from settling. From enjoying the laughter, and the happiness, and the joy, and the *power*.

He saw these people all around him with smiles on their faces. People who'd chosen to follow him. People he'd told of power and who had followed him. And now this was their reward for following him. This was the end of the line for them, as far as they were concerned. This was the treasure at the end of the rainbow. This was what was buried beneath that X that marked the spot.

But not for Yuri.

That fear just wouldn't go away.

He looked around at the community, at the walls, and over at the gates. He could see the trees in the distance, just beyond those gates. The outside world. Big and vast and full of unpredictability, full of surprises, as he knew too well.

And then he sighed. "You're probably right. But make sure if you see them, you do one thing. No questions asked."

"And what's that?" Trent asked.

Yuri took a deep breath and swallowed a lump in his throat. "You shoot on sight."

CHAPTER FORTY-FIVE

"Is this it?" Kayleigh asked.

"Apparently so," Aoife said.

"Phew."

"What?"

"All this power lighting up Sanctuary. All those lights. All that hot water. And this is all that's holding it all. All that's holding all the power."

Aoife nodded. She looked ahead at the metallic green structure right before her. It was unremarkable, to say the least. Green brick. Rusty metal doors.

And a buzz to it.

A buzz of this invisible energy that was so valuable.

An energy that had sparked a war that she'd ended up caught in the middle of.

"Surprised there's not more people guarding the place," Kayleigh said.

"I wouldn't speak too soon."

"Well, either way. We'd better get a move on, hadn't we?"

Aoife looked around at Kayleigh. At Rex, right by her side. And then she looked at the rest of the people who were joining them. Survivors. Survivors from the attack on Sanctuary. About forty of them total. All of them standing with them. Hanging back. Watching.

"I need to do this alone," Aoife said.

Kayleigh shook her head. "Not a chance."

"There's no way we do this with everyone. If something goes wrong, we all fall. We need... we need some way of making sure that doesn't happen."

"A distraction?" Kayleigh said.

"I don't want to call it that. I don't want to use people as bait."

"But that's exactly what you're suggesting. Isn't it?"

Aoife lowered her head. She knew the second she stepped inside the power source that there'd be all kinds of alarms rigged. She knew Yuri's people would be onto them in no time at all.

"I might need... I might need to draw them away from here. Some kind of distraction. To keep the attention off me. If this is really what we're going to do."

Kayleigh shook her head. "You've been down here yourself before. You know exactly where you have to go. The last place we want you is out here using yourself as bait."

"Then what other choice do we have?"

Kayleigh quite visibly swallowed a lump in her throat. "I can cause the distraction."

Aoife shook her head. "Not a chance."

"Someone has to," Kayleigh said. "And if... if you really think this is gonna work. If you really want to strike Yuri in the heart of what he holds dearest, just like I do, then yeah. I happen to think it's worth it. And I'll bet there's plenty of others who think the exact same thing."

Aoife looked at the ground. Shook her head. She couldn't believe what Kayleigh was suggesting. She was suggesting causing some kind of distraction that would allow Aoife to enter the power source. Give her the time she needed to destroy it, once and for all.

"I need you to know something," Aoife said. "About... about both of us. About what this means for us."

"You don't have to say it," Kayleigh said, putting a finger to her lips. "I already know exactly what you're going to say."

Aoife nodded. She knew Kayleigh understood. Where they were going—where both of them were going—there was a good chance they weren't going to come back.

Aoife wasn't sure she was going to make it out of the power source alive.

And she wasn't sure Kayleigh was going to survive acting as a distraction, either.

"We get the rest of the people somewhere safe. Somewhere far away. For now, at least. And then we start."

Someone stepped up. A man. Ben, he was called. Always very vocal. Stubborn old git. Aoife never really gelled with him. But he was here, and he was standing with her and Kayleigh, and that had to count for something.

"You can try your damnedest to make us get somewhere safe," Ben said. "But the truth is... this is our home. People died. Friends died to this Yuri guy. I'm not gonna hide in the shadows while you two try and destroy him. None of us are."

Aoife shook her head. She wanted to stand up to him, wanted to argue.

But then she saw them all standing beside him.

All of them. Every single person from Sanctuary, regardless of age, gender... all of them were standing there. Like they were a united force.

"We're going to get our home back," Ben said. "Power or no power. And we're gonna help you take down the man who took it from us."

Aoife looked at them all. Looked at all these people, led by Kayleigh.

She felt a lump in her throat at their loyalty. Felt like crying for ever doubting Harvey, for ever questioning his legacy.

She took a deep breath, and she nodded at Kayleigh.

"Then you go," she said. "You go, and you do what you need to do."

Kayleigh nodded back. Looked pretty tearful herself.

She took a few steps back. Went to walk away.

And then she walked right up to Aoife and kissed her, right on the lips.

She pulled back. Aoife felt a spark inside her. A fire ignited inside.

"What..."

"I love you, Aoife. I love you, you blind, stubborn idiot. Now go and destroy that power source. Words I never fucking thought I'd say."

Aoife smiled. The warmth inside her growing warmer and warmer.

"I love you too," she said.

She looked at those people. That crowd of people, all here to work with her, all ready to run to her aid.

And then she took a deep breath, and she turned around.

It was time to go into the power source.

It was time to destroy the electricity.

It was time to end this, once and for—

Gunshot.

Shouts.

"They're here!"

Aoife's skin went cold.

It was already too late.

Yuri's people were here.

CHAPTER FORTY-SIX

Aoife heard the gunfire and the shouts, and she knew she was already too late.

Yuri's people were already here.

They were already here, and the people of Sanctuary were under attack.

Time was running out.

She stood there in the front of this crowd. Saw them turning around. Half-expected them to start running. Start fleeing. Start bolting for their lives and dispersing.

But they didn't.

They stood their ground.

Stood shoulder to shoulder and fought back.

Like they were trying to stop Yuri's people getting through to Aoife.

Like suddenly, her goal, her urgency to destroy the power they once held central to their entire lives, was now the most important thing in the world.

More important even than their lives as individuals.

She looked around, and she lifted her pistol. She wanted to stand up and fight with them. She didn't want to leave them. Not again. Not after everything that had happened. And not after the amount of time she'd walked away from situations like this in the past, from people like this in the past.

Not after being so responsible for so many deaths in the past.

But as she stepped forward, Kayleigh pushed her back.

"Kayleigh?"

Kayleigh had a look of concern on her wide-eyed face. "You need to go."

"But I—"

"You're only gonna get one shot at this. One fucking shot. If you don't go now, we'll be dying for nothing. You've got to go. You've got to try. You have to."

Aoife couldn't move. She shook her head. Tears welling up. "I can't leave you."

"You're not leaving us," Kayleigh said, putting a soft hand to her face. "We're choosing to be here. We're choosing to fight for this. Because it's what we believe in."

Aoife heard the shouting. She heard the cries. She heard the sound of conflict, of war, of people she knew dying, and of people she knew fighting for what they believed in, and she didn't want to abandon them. She didn't want to leave them.

But then Kayleigh spoke again, and she cut right through Aoife's thoughts.

"You don't have much time. You have one chance at this. Just one. Go. Go, now. And what happens, happens. But if you don't go, if you don't try, you know exactly what happens. Would you rather have that on your conscience than the alternative?"

Aoife felt sickness. Sickness, right within. She shook her head. "I don't want to walk away."

"You're not walking away," Kayleigh said. "You're doing exactly what you need to do. What we all know needs to be done."

She looked at Kayleigh.

Then at the wall of people beyond, barely any cracks in their chain.

She turned around to the metal doors of the power source.

So close.

So, so close.

"We're with you," Kayleigh said. "Me and Rex are with you. Every damned step of the way. We always have been. Even that night in the club two years ago when I was trying to hook you up with someone but secretly feeling jealous of him."

Aoife laughed and cried. She laughed and cried as she looked down at Rex, wagging his tail despite the chaos unfolding all around him. She laughed and cried as Kayleigh cried too.

And then she looked her in the eye, knowing full well time was running out, and she forced herself to smile.

"Thank you," Aoife said.

"For what?"

"For making me remember there is hope."

She kissed her back, right on the lips.

Then she turned around.

Ran towards the metal doors of the power supply.

Landed against them with a slam as gunfire and shouting filled her surroundings.

Tried to yank them open, struggling to pull them apart, struggling to break them free.

"Come on," she said. "Come on!"

She heard Rex barking behind. She heard the gunshots and the cries getting closer. She didn't want to look back. She couldn't look back.

She had to focus on herself.

On breaking these doors open.

On getting inside.

"Please," she gasped. "Please."

She yanked at the doors with the last of her strength, the last of her energy, and prepared herself to just fall to the ground.

But this time, the doors opened.

They opened, and she felt the warmth from inside.

Heard the hum of the power right before her.

She stared into that abyss. Like she was staring into the jaws of hell.

And she stepped inside.

She looked around. Just once.

The last thing she saw before she closed the doors was Kayleigh staring right back at her, smile on her tear-soaked face, Rex right by her side.

She forced a smile at her.

And then she slammed the doors shut.

CHAPTER FORTY-SEVEN

Aoife turned around from the power source doors and looked ahead.

She knew exactly what she had to do now and where she needed to go.

It was dark in here. A hum to the air. The hum of electricity. Of power.

So inviting. So warm. The very thing she and so many people valued more than anything. The very thing that humanity had lost and the very thing that had sent society spiralling out of control completely.

Here. Right here.

The source of it.

The source of a new beginning.

And she was going to just destroy it?

It felt wrong.

And yet...

She remembered what Kayleigh said. What so many more people from Sanctuary said. It wasn't electricity or power that was the most important thing. It was community and connection.

Because power, when it had fallen into the wrong hands, could be used as a tool. As a bargaining chip. As a way of one group ruling over another.

Yuri had made her believe it was Harvey who was doing that.

And it turned out it was the exact opposite.

She had to take away what he valued most before he could even begin enjoying it.

She stepped forwards, towards the ladder. Looked down into the darkness. Held her pistol tight in hand. She knew what she had to do. Where she needed to go. Down.

Follow the wires down.

Make it to the core.

And then she had to destroy this place.

She went to start climbing the ladders down when she heard a few bullets outside bang against the door.

She looked back. Heard the voices and the shouting getting closer. She had to be fast. She didn't have all day. It wouldn't be long before Yuri and his people were onto her through the door.

She didn't have long at all, and she had to make the head start she had count.

She clambered down the ladder. Further and further into the darkness. The ladder stretched on longer than she remembered. And the darkness was intense, suffocating, like no darkness she'd ever experienced.

She should have brought a torch down with her.

But she couldn't start worrying about what she had or hadn't done.

She kept on climbing down the ladder, kept on going further and further into the darkness, getting further away from the shouting and the gunfire outside when finally, she reached the floor.

She stopped when she reached the bottom. Turned around into the dark. Looked right ahead. She knew it was up front. Knew where she needed to go.

She started to run when suddenly she heard a bang above.

She looked up. The muffled sounds outside suddenly became closer, more audible.

She looked up the void she'd just climbed down and saw the flicker of torchlight.

"Down the ladders!" someone shouted. "She's down there!"

Fuck.

She ran. Ran as fast as she could, while behind her, she heard those boots clambering down the ladders. Heard the sound of heavy feet on metal, one after another.

She kept on running. It was all she could do. She couldn't look back. She had to just keep going.

She ran and ran, and then she slammed into a wall.

She stopped. It was so dark she couldn't see a thing. And she was forgetting whether it was a left or a right turn here. She couldn't remember. Shit. Shit.

But she had to be fast.

Because suddenly, light illuminated the corridor.

She took a left and right on cue; bullets hit the wall right where she'd stood.

Fuck.

They were here, now.

They were here, and she'd committed to turning left.

In for a penny, in for a pound.

She ran down this corridor. Heard the boots echoing behind her. Saw a few glimmers of light. She started to worry that she'd taken a wrong turn. And if she had, she was screwed. She'd blown it. Completely blown it.

She kept on going anyway, knowing it was her only choice.

And suddenly, she hit a wall.

She froze. Her stomach sank. She'd made a wrong turn. She'd made a wrong turn, and they were going to be on to her. They were going to reach her, and they were going to kill her, and this would all be for nothing.

She went to turn around to look back when suddenly she felt something protruding from the wall.

Something that made her realise it wasn't a wall at all.

It was a handle.

A door handle.

She turned the handle, and then nothing happened.

Nothing, and then: PASSWORD REQUIRED.

Shit. Password? She didn't remember anything about a password.

Footsteps getting closer.

Light getting closer.

She tried the handle again.

Nothing.

And that robotic woman's voice. "PASSWORD REQUIRED."

She closed her eyes. Her stomach dropped. A password? She had no clue. Absolutely no clue. She should have known something like this would stand in her way. She should have seen this coming.

She lowered her head, closed her eyes, when suddenly a spark of inspiration came to mind.

"Ben and Ross," she said. Harvey's kids. Could it be?

She tried the handle.

Then she said those words again as the footsteps and the light got closer, closer.

"Ben and Ross," she said. "Ross and Ben. Ben and Ross!"

She waited.

Nothing.

And then: "ACCESS GRANTED."

The door clicked.

The handle lowered.

And then the door opened.

She stepped inside, slamming the door behind her.

Right ahead of her, she saw it.

It was small. Wires all worming out of it. Only about six feet high. Grey metal, with a slight illumination from above.

But there was no doubting what this was.

The power core.

She knew it was different. Electricity worked differently these days, according to the Order of Light. She didn't know how it worked. She didn't know how they'd managed to restore power in the first place, let alone activate something like this—using technology that was many, many years ahead of its time, apparently.

She just knew she had to destroy it.

Because electricity wasn't where real power rested.

And in Yuri's hands... he could become tyrannical.

He could become the most powerful man in the country.

She walked over to it.

Opened the door at the front of it, hands shaking.

Tore off chunks of metal protecting it.

And then she lifted her pistol.

Pointed it at it.

For a second, as she stood there, no sounds from outside anymore, she wondered if this was the right thing to do.

She wondered whether this was selfish. Whether she wasn't really considering the future of humanity at all. But putting her and *her* people first.

But then she took a deep breath.

Shook her head.

She knew what she had to do.

She went to pull the trigger when suddenly, the door behind her clicked, and she heard footsteps.

"I wouldn't do that if I were you," a voice said.

Aoife turned.

Yuri stood there.

A ton of his people by his side. Guns pointed at Aoife.

And in front of Yuri, gun to her head, Kayleigh.

CHAPTER FORTY-EIGHT

"It ends here, Aoife. Right here. Right now. Step away from the power source, or I'll be forced to kill her. You don't want that. None of us want that. Right?"

Aoife stood right by the power source. She still had her pistol pointed at it. Still had her finger tightly wrapped around the trigger. She knew she had the power to end all this right now. To bring down the power charging this place up. To end it, once and for all.

But at the same time, she knew that doing so would result in Kayleigh's death. And it would result in her death, too.

She looked around at the torchlights surrounding her. The torchlights of Yuri's people. She looked at each and every one of them, holding those rifles. And then at Kayleigh. Standing there with that pistol to her head. Staring right at Aoife. She didn't look afraid. She didn't look tearful. She looked... strangely calm.

"Come on," Yuri said. "This has gone way too far. I should have known you'd be trouble. I should have known you'd find a way to get back at me. But let's just say I didn't account for the possibility you might actually survive that blast."

Aoife shook her head. "You lied to me. You lied about everything."

"Harvey was a ghastly monster of a man," Yuri said. "But the fact he was who he was... really, it was just an added bonus. Because Sanctuary, as you call it, was always destined to fall into our hands eventually."

"Who are you people?" Aoife asked.

Yuri shrugged. Smiled a little. The first time she'd seen that stony, stoic face break into something more narcissistic and psychopathic than ever before. "Who I am doesn't matter. What matters is this place is ours now. And it will continue to be ours. And people will flock here. They will flock to us, and they will kneel before us, and we will protect them. And if they don't... well. Every world needs some order, doesn't it? And what better way to convince people to join our side than with electricity itself."

Aoife shook her head. She had no idea what to say. Only that all her worst fears about Yuri abusing his power were proving correct.

"I've no doubt you'll have a lot of questions," Yuri said, standing there in the darkness. Pistol firmly pointed at Kayleigh. "And there's only one way I'll answer them. Step away from that power source right now. Lower your pistol and step away. Because you don't want this. Destroying the power source? Really? The very thing you and your people have spent so long enjoying? The very thing so many people have worked so hard to build and install? The very hope of the future of mankind? Really?"

Aoife kept her pistol pointed right at that power source. "It was good when we had it," she said. "Harvey... Harvey was a good man. And he wanted everyone to enjoy it. But now it's fallen into your hands. And as long as it's around, there's a chance it might fall into the hands of people like yours."

"And who are you to decide whose hands it's allowed to fall

into?" he asked. "Who are you to decide whether I am any better or worse a person to run a community?"

"It's not just my decision," Aoife said. "You're right about that. But what you've done. What you've done to so many people of mine. Innocent people—"

"And you think you've done much better?" Yuri snapped. "You really think you're all innocent? That we haven't lost innocent people, too?"

"You're a snake," Aoife said. "You're a snake, and you're full of shit. Completely full of shit. This all started because of what you did to Harvey's children. This all started because of your grudge. I know how strong revenge can be. But I know the difference between acting in vengeance and acting out of evil and spite. You've slaughtered people. You've slaughtered people, and you've got your entire community of followers to worship you as some kind of leader. Well, it's over, Yuri. It's over. I've dealt with enough psychopathic leaders to know when I'm dealing with another. It ends. If I have to destroy the power source to take away the very thing these people worship you for... if I have to destroy the only thing that gives you any kind of power over the rest of the country, well, the house of cards will soon come toppling down; let's put it that way."

Yuri stared at her. And for the first time, he looked genuinely concerned. Like he was worried.

He yanked Kayleigh closer. Pushed that pistol deep into her skull. "If you step away, and if you lower that pistol, I'll let her live. And I'll let you live too."

"You expect me to believe that after everything? We're as good as dead already."

"I don't expect you to believe me. But I give you my word. And it's about the only thing I can give you right now."

Aoife gritted her teeth. Looked at Kayleigh, right into her eyes.

"Think about it," Yuri said. "Think about the millions of

potential lives that this power could enrich. I'm not saying you'll have the best life. I'm not saying I'll give you a life of luxury. But you will be viewed kindly in history by our people for making this choice. For choosing not to shoot. So think about it. Very, very carefully."

Aoife stood there. Hand shaking. She shook her head. Fear crept up. Anxiety taking hold.

She looked at Kayleigh. At Yuri. She looked at all these people with their torchlights shining at her. She wanted time. Time to think. Time to figure out what the fuck she was going to do.

"Put the pistol down," Yuri said. "Put it down, and it ends. Put it down, and you live. Both of you live."

She looked right at Kayleigh again. Right into her eyes. She didn't want to watch her die. She didn't want to watch her skull explode. She didn't want to watch her fall to the floor.

But she saw the intensity with which Kayleigh stared right at her.

Saw the way she nodded.

And she knew exactly what she had to do.

She knew what Kayleigh would say.

She knew this was bigger than just the pair of them.

She knew this was for her community.

"There's one thing more important than power," Aoife said.

Yuri frowned. "And what's that?"

Aoife lifted her pistol. "Connection."

She pointed at the power source.

Held her breath.

Closed her eyes.

And she pulled the trigger.

* * *

END OF BOOK 6

Fight For Darkness, the seventh book in the Survive the Darkness series, is now available.

If you want to be notified when Ryan Casey's next novel is released—and receive an exclusive post apocalyptic novel totally free—sign up for the author newsletter: ryancaseybooks.com/fanclub

www.ingramcontent.com/pod-product-compliance
Lightning Source LLC
Chambersburg PA
CBHW060535160726
47991CB00001B/338